Philosophical Investigations

Steve Attridge

© Steve Attridge 2013

Steve Attridge has asserted his rights under the Copyright, Design and Patents Act, 1988, to be identified as the author of this work.

First published in 2013 by Endeavour Press Ltd.

This edition published 2014 by Createspace.

For my Mother, Jake, Hedda and Tom.

Chapter I

'When you look long into an abyss, the abyss looks into you.'

Nietzsche

I walk around the supermarket, dividing things into three categories: fatal, near fatal and tasteless. I also plan the murder of my best friend, David, and invent a new illness to avoid going to work. I call it moroniphobia – a fatal aversion to idiots. My head of department, Jeremy, a man of few parts, none of them working, will use it as another spanner to try and lever me out. It's hard to sack an academic, especially one who does so little, like me – how can they find fault with what doesn't exist? Our horns are locked and I am now determined he will fail which will drive him closer to the breakdown he so deserves, and even this will be an indifferent, mousey affair. Travel back with me three months and you'll understand the vehemence of my Jeremy project. He asks me to resign. I refuse. A week later I am summoned to a disciplinary hearing where Jeremy accuses me of propositioning a young female student. She is so anxious, he says, growing dewy eyed and sincere, that she does not wish to appear herself, or even be named, and as Head of Department, he must protect her confidentiality. Of course, she doesn't exist. I am given a formal warning, nothing more, but mud sticks, as Jeremy knows. That was the moment I decided to destroy him.

I am not naturally bleak; it's a view I worked hard to attain and constantly fine tune, a view emanating from a settled conviction that the darkest thinkers are the most joyful: we have no illusions and can gleefully dissect the world with our cynical little scalpels. I settle on a bottle of Rioja, another of Famous Grouse and some Applewood cheese and grissini. At the checkout a bleached angel with bad skin, a lip piercing that makes her look like a hooked herring, and a nametag that says her thin chest is called Stacey, asks if I need help.

"I think I'm beyond it," I say.

"With packing," she says, no flicker of irony or recognition.

I know what she is looking at. A middle aged man with circles under his eyes, scuffed leather jacket, tallish, thin. I could add: rakishly attractive, enigmatically self destructive, oozing sex, but even I wouldn't believe it. Some things I am very good at, but they don't endear me to the human race. Then I get a call that distracts me from my self obsessing. Not just any call, but from the most dangerous man in England. Psychotic, unwired, voice like a South London box of pins, the charm of a tarantula in a children's party hat. God is in his coffin and all is wrong with the world. His name is Tony Steele, or Tony the Blade as he likes to be called, and he is a son in the principal crime family in South England. They make the Borgias look like soap fairies. Tony once nailed an enemy to motorway tarmac. It was the only corpse in police records to be found in three different counties.

"Five o'clock. The Castle. Directions follow in an email. Don't be late. It's about an hour away from you."

Leave at four. That means cutting my three o'clock seminar down to half an hour. Bliss. On the drive into the discount warehouse that thinks it's a university I ponder what the Steeles would want with me. No point in wondering if it is safe to go to the Castle, their family home; that would be like asking if it is safe to invite a pyromaniac to a firework party. You need to know why they would even ring me in the first place – a disgruntled, self pitying middle aged man lost in the past and drowning in the present, more inert coward than action hero. I am like a bat: my real life is in the dark. I am ostensibly a disgruntled philosophy lecturer, but I am also Rook Investigations – a private investigator. Look me up in the Yellow Pages and you won't find me. I only work for those who don't want the police involved, and that usually means criminals, or at least people with secrets. But here's another contradiction – I am addicted to danger. It is one of the side effects of a path I chose some years ago. Nothing comes for free. I thought that by becoming a shadow in the underworld I would find someone I desperately need to meet – my father – but so far I have only found other shadows, and like reaching for the bottle I need a constant fix of danger. An odd and pathetic addiction for a coward, but then consistency was never my forte. Perhaps that's why my wife Lizzie skewered my love on a kebab stick. I shouldn't blame her, but I do. It's easier.

I finish the seminar early by upsetting a student – always a good ploy. On the whiteboard I scrawled "GOD IS MY FAVOURITE FICTIONAL CHARACTER" and asked who said that. No one got it. Homer said it. Homer Simpson. A girl with a pinched face and a mouth like a hairpin looked upset, and asked why I said something derogatory about Christianity every week. I said that I must be slipping if it was only weekly, and that if God was upset with me then he should complain in person and not send sad teenage envoys. It isn't Christianity that upsets me; it is religious piety that makes me want to gun down baby ducks.

"Do you want to be a myrmidon all your life?" I ask her.

"I don't even know what that means," she says, her neck flushing behind her silver cross.

"Then spend less time in church and more thumbing through a dictionary. It'll do your soul more good."

I am being a complete bastard but it has to be done. Ultimately it's an act of Mercy. The atmosphere soured and I sent everyone off to the library, which means they'll all sit in the refectory gawping at apps on their smart phones.

Only one student remained. I suppose she had a right to. She's my daughter, sometimes my keeper. The lovely, impossible, annoying, full of light and razorblades, Cass. My soon to be ex-wife Lizzie also looks out of her cornflower eyes, which squeezes my heart into a tight ball of madness.

Lizzie is a sitting tenant in what used to be my mind.

"Why do you do it?" She asks. "If you get sacked you'll be even more miserable."

I smile and start to pack up. Was it just due to serendipity that I was teaching my own daughter? Did she really forget to sign up for her Phil 1 options and be forced to take mine – "Fictions of Evil" – thankfully the least popular course in the whole department? Less essays, less students. Or is she up to something?

"I saw Mum last night."

She was up to something.

"Sharpening her broomstick? Putting pins in my effigy?"

"Dad, that is so childish."

She was right. I am ridiculous, but unlike most, I know it. The elephant in the room is David, MP for Nuneaton. Idealistic, intelligent, now humping my wife on a regular basis. When I imagine them – as I frequently do – my mind feels like a blister. Much of my dreamtime is spent on exactly how I can arrange his death. It's possible. I know a lot of strange people who need money and like the action.

"I wish I didn't feel so anxious about you," she said.

"Read your Heidegger. 'Mere anxiety' is at the source of everything."

"I hate it when you're smug."

"I love it when you're annoyed," I said, and kissed her cheek.

In the car park Jeremy flounced up to me, with florid cheeks and waving a piece of paper. He looked close to a heart attack.

"What the hell is this?" He hissed.

"Piece of paper, Jeremy."

"It's your assessment form. Your bloody assessment of the Faculty, which means of me. The Vice Chancellor was on the phone to me at eight o'clock this morning. Wanting to know if any of it was true."

"And is it?"

He purpled. Surely the pump would give way any moment now.

"You wrote the bloody thing. The VC wants to know why a member of this faculty would say I am a practicing Druid and that I am not...", and here he read, "...in principle, against either bestiality or incest."

"Very liberal of you, Jeremy."

"Your juvenile lunacies have gone far enough. I would like you to resign."

"I can't. I need the salary. I suggest you go home, get Mrs. Jeremy to pour you a nice big glass of supermarket sherry, and listen to your Bobby Crush tapes. You need to relax."

He wanted to kill me. How far must I go before he actually tries? As an experiment it was almost interesting. He's not a formidable opponent, but he will be good practise and he's a bully. Worse still, he's mediocre.

Time to go. I had a date with a different kind of devil.

Chapter II

'There are certain clues at a crime scene which, by their very nature, do not lend themselves to being collected or examined. How does one collect love, rage, hatred, fear…? These are things that we're trained to look for.'

James Reese

The Steeles were old school. Pop Steele had been a South London crime gang soldier – gambling, protection, robbery, but unlike most criminals, he could see the big picture and planned for the future. Worked his way up inch by inch, blow by blow, pound by pound, deal by deal, risk by risk, matching streetwise savvy, natural flair and an instinct for survival against rivals and what are dizzily called the forces of law and order. Before anyone knew it he had an empire. You can't build an empire without drugs, that's where the big money is, but Pop was clever enough to keep it all at a distance and pay others to do the deals, take the risks. It was a calculated payoff and it worked. Now his legitimate business interests were so bound up with his criminal ones that it would take a galaxy of criminal lawyers to unpick them. As he once said when he'd eeled his slippery way out of an injunction: "There's only the business of crime and the crime of business."

Little did he know that the enemy was always within. Pop had carefully planned how to keep outside threats at bay, but his world was in turmoil because of those closest to him – his children. They were a national soap opera, much to Pop's chagrin: Jimbo, clever but burnt out and wired, Tony the psycho, Philly the wayward daughter, a son who died in a car crash years ago, and Danny, recently murdered, though details had been withheld. I suspected that's why I'd been summoned. The Steeles would not embrace a police investigation. At an age when Pop was doubtless hoping to enjoy good wine and afternoon naps he was trying to control this wayward bunch and stop his world imploding. His wife, Ma Steele, a bulldog of a woman who showed that you could take the woman out of a Bermondsey slum, but not...you know the rest, protected Pop in her own inimitable way, but some thought family cracks were spreading fast. I'd soon be able to decide for myself.

The offensively opulent Castle had more CCTV cameras than a presidential palace. I smiled and felt the familiar cold prickle of excitement that accompanied entering the lion's den. Like going on stage, I imagine, but with infinitely more at stake. Excited and shit scared, the possibility of not returning. Nothing so simple as a death wish, more an embracing of uncertainty and the adrenalin rush of knowing you cannot control events. The boxer chooses to go in the ring but does not wish to get hurt, which is a likely outcome of going into the ring. We are all bee boxes of contradictions. I can go on like this for hours.

Gold tipped iron gates, a driveway long enough to land a Boeing 707. A front door the size of a small bungalow and framed by Corinthian pillars, opened as I approached the house which stood like a giant wedding cake; inside were Rococo architraves, rooms you needed a taxi to cross and the hall had a ludicrous ceiling fresco of the whole family as Olympian figures. My guess was that this was not Pop's doing, nor Ma's, but a result of the gargantuan ego of Tony. As Jimbo, all sugared up burnt out energy in a bomber jacket and jogging bottoms, showed me in, he smiled as I looked up and took in the full tastelessness of the thing.

"Load of crap, that's what Pop thinks. Ma tried to scrub it off. Tony's idea. Had it done while we was at the villa in Portugal." Bingo. I'm nearly always right except when I'm wrong.

Jimbo took me into a sitting room kaleidoscopically lit by the setting sun through stained glass windows. There were five sofas, six clocks and eight expensive rugs on a marble tiled floor. I count things – it's one of my many compulsive disorders. Already this place was wearying me with its tacky and stifling opulence.

We sat. I realised that Jimbo had been given the twin job of putting me in the picture and appraising me before I was allowed to see the King of this little sugar pile.

"Know why you're here?" asked Jimbo, his knee jerking up and down.

"To find out who killed your brother," I said.

"Shot and trussed up like a bleedin' chicken. Pop had a bit of a turn when he saw him."

He gave me a photograph of a corpse bandaged like a mummy in an old raincoat, and I counted blood from ten gunshots staining the material. I had a ton of questions but now wasn't the moment to ask.

"Some basket with a death wish trying to show us his meat and two veg is bigger than ours," said Jimbo. "You up for it?"

"That's why I'm here," I said, smiling.

"OK, lift off. Four ton a day plus expenses, Pop says."

"I'll take a hundred a day. Pay my own expenses."

Jimbo looked at me curiously. No one turned down money. I smiled again, knowing I was being watched on at least one monitor somewhere in the house. Two cameras in opposite corners of the room.

"It's my proletarian roots. Plus, it makes me feel as if I've negotiated the deal and not you and your family," I said.

He liked this. The face cracked a large smile. "They said you was a bit of a ding-a-ling. If you want peanuts, we'll chuck 'em. Done deal. "

I wasn't being modest, but pragmatic. If you get greedy you get hasty, and also your employer thinks he owns you. I wanted at least the illusion of exercising some control. I'd been vetted, and as though he'd received some electronic signal Jimbo sparked to his feet and told me to follow him; up a Bollywood musical staircase to the first floor. We entered a drawing room lined with leather sofas. I quickly scanned fifteen pictures on the wall, mostly of Pop Steele shaking hands with Establishment figures: Chief of Police; a judge; Archbishop of

Canterbury. One thing about England today – everyone is in bed with everyone else. In one corner was Philly, the daughter. She looked like the horny side of Soho, about thirty, danger to mankind, thickset but sexy. In the other corner was Tony – his face showing what lurked beneath: the stew of cocaine, sadism and terror that made him a psychopath. In front of me, sitting incongruously on a char's wooden stall, was Ma, legs apart and hands on knees, thick black woollen stockings and a cheap black dress. Built like a navvy. Desperate Dan chin. This was not a woman to cross. She and Pop had met when in their teens and been a formidable team ever since.

"This is the Rook bloke, Ma," said Jimbo.

"Looks more like a shithouse rat to me," said Ma.

"It's nice to meet you too, Mrs Steele."

Jimbo indicated Tony, who just stared at me, and Philly nodded, puffing furiously on a B&H.

"And when do I have the pleasure of meeting Mr Steele?"

"Later," said Ma. "You got one week to find who killed my son. It's important things are done quick and clean in our family. I promised Danny Boy he'd get justice."

I looked at her curiously.

"In my prayers I told him. So's he can lie peaceful, forgetful of all ill. Where'd you want to start?"

"I'd like to talk to you individually," I said, but then things happened quickly. Tony's phone beeped, he shot me a glance of pure hatred, got up and left the room. There was a lot of noise coming up the stairs. Then a dark suited muscleman with a neck as thick as a postbox brought a young girl in, arm locked. She winced as he tightened his grip. Tony looked at me. I had no doubt he and the muscleman were armed. I looked at the girl and she at me. It was my daughter. Cass. Shit.

Chapter III

'Evil is unspectacular, and always human, and shares our bed and eats at our table.'

W. H. Auden

"Snooping around the fence. Says she knows Einstein here," said Tony, indicating me with a perfectly manicured hand. I swear I could detect nail gloss.

Ma looked at me coolly. "And do you?" she asked.

I nodded. I often look at my most calm when I have the screaming terrors.

"So why would you 'ave some girl snooping around our place?"

"I told you this was a mistake. We can sort this ourselves without some greasy choad and his nosy tart," said Tony.

Cass was scared but trying not to show it in the tight lipped face she used to wear as a little girl after I'd read her a bedtime story and then she knew she'd have to face the dark alone. No matter how often we told her there was nothing to fear, she dreaded the nights. I ached to make everything all right for her then as now. It was vital to remain uber calm. I decided that a half truth was the best, if least plausible, option. Especially because someone as thorough as Pop must already have done some sort of background check on me – for all I knew he'd have seen photographs of Cass. If things got nasty I would first try to talk our way out of it – always the best option – failing that I'd say that in fact I was working for the police and they knew both Cass and I were there – failing that I would either fake a fit or run headlong at the muscle giant and hope Cass had at least a chance to run. I had told Cass my interest in the underworld was academic, a strange intellectual fetish. Now she must be bursting with questions, all sensibly held in check by fear.

"This is my daughter, Cass. She needed money for a train fare to London for some research she's doing. Sorry, Cass. I just forgot." I took out my wallet and gave her twenty pounds, which she took. Her hand trembled. I wanted to hold her tight. I was also ice and fire angry with her. Why did she follow me? More to the point, why didn't I notice? This was all my stupid fault.

"You think we believe that?" asked Tony, his face zipped into a smirk.

"Research? Into what?" Ma asked.

"Crime and punishment," said Cass quick as a whippet.

There was a silence you could hack through. Then a splutter as Jimbo burst into a giggle. It relaxed Ma, who smiled and saw the joke.

"Big subject, that, my girl. You best get going. Take a bleedin' lifetime."

Tony almost choked. "You're not letting her go. It's mad. She could be anyone."

"We know who she is. And letting her go is exactly what I'm doing. Dino…" – she nodded at the muscleman – "...escort this young person from the premises. She's a good girl, and we don't want her Dad worrying about her." Dino took her arm and I smiled again at her.

"See you later," I said and gave her a kiss on the cheek. It was white with fear. Then she was gone. She would probably be sick when she got outside. I hoped she wouldn't tell Lizzie. You never knew with Cass. She could be as independent as the sun one moment and little girl lost the next. But why why why had she followed me? I was aware the sides of my nose were beaded with sweat but to wipe it away would be to acknowledge it.

"Does she know why you're here?" Ma asked.

"No. As you said, she's a good girl. She doesn't ask too many questions," I lied.

"He's lying. The nonce is lying," said Tony.

"Then the nonce will be sorry," said Ma.

All this time Philly had sat in a corner watching, like a damaged bird of prey. She'd smoked three cigarettes. What the hell had I got into?

An internal phone rang. Ma picked it up, listened, and returned it to its holster.

"Praise the lord, 'is Whiskers is up and breathing and wants to see you."

As I passed Tony I could smell expensive aftershave. Gucci or one those crappy designer names that puts a logo on cheap perfume and multiplies the price by fifty. I imagined Tony's mind as a Thames sludge pool with evil things fermenting and hatching in the mud's poisonous gases. But Cass was safe – that was all that mattered. Now the crisis was over I could feel something deep in me churning with what might have beens. What am I doing?

*

A dark bedroom with curtains drawn, a few wall lights, and maps everywhere: on walls, propped up against shelves, even one of the world on the ceiling, a large revolving globe lit from within on a circular mahogany table, the legs carved like dolphins. There was a large glass ornament, like a cloud, on the floor. Pop Steele was in a wheelchair, eyes closed, and listening to the radio shipping forecast. Odd time for a shipping forecast – they usually came early or late. He was unshaven, wearing a dressing gown, his swollen ankles oozing over tartan slippers. His lips moved in synch with the announcer's voice: "There are warnings of gales in Rockall, Hebrides, Bailey, Fair isle, Faeroes and Southeast Iceland..." One eye drooped slightly and there was a slight downturn of his left lower lip. Mild stroke, but you could see he was tough. It would take more than lightning to the brain and a hammer to the heart to down this old turkey.

"My name is Rook," I said somewhat unnecessarily. He indicated a seat. I sat. The announcer droned on: "Viking North Utrise variable, mainly northwest, becoming north east five to seven, perhaps gale eight in North Viking...", then Pop turned down the sound.

"I didn't know you were a nautical man," I said.

"Fisher German Bright Westerly three or four," he said, then turned up the volume and the announcer said the exact same words. He turned it down and said "South Utrise Cromarty Forth Tyne Dogger Variable three," and turned up the volume. Again the announcer repeated the same words. Either Pop was a mystic or it wasn't a radio, it was a recording and Pop had learnt it all by heart. He smiled.

"June 13th, nineteen eighty three. One of my favourites."

"You record the shipping forecasts and learn them by heart?" I asked.

He indicated a shelf that had hundreds of CDs.

"Soothing, the names. Poetry. Like praying."

"You believe in God?"

"Probably not. I believe in the weather. Oceans. You're here to try and find my son's killer."

"Yes. Any idea who it might be?"

Pop picked up a copy of the telephone directory and threw it at me. I got the point.

"We need a neutral. Someone who might see something because we're too close to be able to. I'm tired, Mister Rook. I was wild once. Not now. Now I enjoy the wine but I want others to pick the grapes."

We stopped and listened to the shipping forecast for a while. Dogger Bank. Humber Thames Dover. I was beginning to see the point of it.

"If I start to think you're wasting my time you need to worry, Mister Rook." He looked at me closely. "Tell me what you've discovered about me since you came in this room." Another test.

"You're not well, but you're strong. You're a watcher, especially when creating the impression you're doing something else – I came in the room and you had your eyes almost closed and ignored me, but you were watching. An observer – I suspect that's partly why you've been so spectacularly successful. You notice things other people don't – weaknesses, mannerisms, hesitations, tiny holes in the mask. You often dispense with verbs. Twice you used sentences containing only a noun. Suggests you like to cut to the chase..."

He raised a hand to stop me. "And what have you worked out about Tony?"

"He's a live wire."

"I meant the truth."

"He's a psychotic monster. Useful on occasions but a colossal liability. You're probably very worried about what will happen to the family when..."

"My ashes are floating down the Thames," he finished for me.

Telling the truth about Tony was a calculated risk; and it worked. Pop smiled, but then his face clouded. I saw what the little fish must see just before the shark attack.

"You find whoever it was who killed Danny. He was my favourite. After...never mind. I could have anyone I wanted brought here and have things done to 'em you can't imagine to find out who killed my boy, but half of them would grass anyone up just to stop it, and some would be so scared they'd admit to anything. So it'd be bloody pointless. You find 'em. Otherwise you got me to deal with."

"No pressure then."

"No pressure."

"What gun was used to shoot Danny?"

"Funny that. Old fashioned luger. Like some forties throwback." His mood filled the room, like a vapour. "My wife will have lots of theories. About everything," he said wearily.

"Yes, she doesn't strike me as the retiring type."

Pop smiled. He was starting to like me, against his will. God knows, I needed an ally in this family. "Congratulations. You spot a domestic rift. In fact she's listening right now, outside the door. Are you married?"

"Technically. Separated. Polite word for crucifixion."

He looked at me. We both felt someone listening outside.

"I'm still head of the family. Ma knows that. For thirty years I brought home the bacon that made her fat. I did things...now get out and do your job, Mister Rook. Moderate or poor, becoming cyclonic..." And he turned up the volume. I'd been dismissed.

Chapter IV

'From the deepest desires often come the deadliest hate.'

Socrates.

Ma was standing outside the room. She made no attempt to hide the fact she'd been listening.

"'E likes you, but I don't," she said.

"Can't win 'em all," I said.

"Never did like posh bastards."

"I was born in Hornsey."

"Jimbo said you're a philosopher or something. What the bloody 'ell use is philosophy when it's at 'ome?"

"It gives you something to do when the scotch is gone."

This delightful meeting of minds was interrupted by a scream. For a woman the size of a small buffalo Ma could move fast and was off down the hall. I followed.

Philly was wrapped only in a fluffy pink towel, dripping wet and looking at Jimbo with a mix of fury and shock. The Dooley Wilson *Casablanca* version of *As Time Goes By* was playing too loudly. Philly snapped it off and glared at Jimbo.

"What the crap are you playing at?"

Jimbo flushed.

"What 'appened?" asked Ma.

"I'm in the shower and this idiot comes in and stuffs Belinda down the toilet, then puts a CD on. Trying to scare me."

I went to the bathroom, expecting to find a drowned cat, but it was a doll stuffed head first, her little legs sticking out from green frilly pants like two chubby plastic sausages. The shower was still running and I turned it off. On the shower glass wall was a silhouetted black painted profile of the knife wielding 'mother' from the *Psycho* shower scene. Philly was an alarming potpourri of little girl lost, modern vamp and weirdo. She liked Dooley

Wilson, so she couldn't be all bad. I took the doll from the toilet. Its mouth had been slit and a piece of paper folded in it. Although wet, I could open it. A newspaper photograph of the Steele family, taken a few years ago when Pop was still mobile, at some sort of gala dinner, all looking prosperous and pleased with themselves. I took a small plastic bag from a shelf and put the picture inside, washed my hands, then rejoined the happy family – just warming up for the heavy artillery. If ever there was a family on the verge of implosion, this was it.

"I heard you scream – that's why I came in!" said Jimbo.

"Bollocks!" said Philly.

Ma slapped her. "Language, missy. No wonder you can't keep a man."

Philly gave her a look of pure hatred, then went back in the bathroom and slammed the door.

"It bloody wasn't me. She's my sister," said Jimbo.

A window was slightly open. I went to it and looked out. A drop of five metres to a lawn below.

About fifteen metres away Tony emerged from a densely shrubbed garden, brushing leaves from his suit. He looked up and saw me.

"Thought I saw someone. Everyone all right?" he asked.

I nodded. What was going on here? A brother spooking a sister? But which brother? Or maybe neither.

"We need more security. I'll get some people in," said Jimbo.

"You must think us a model family, Mister Rook."

It was Pop, silently arrived in his electric wheelchair, at the door.

"I was saying, Pop. We need to be careful," said Jimbo.

"Never miss an opportunity to state the bleedin' obvious, eh Jimbo? It's not just a question of watching our backs and getting muscle in as protection. We need to think. That's why I got an extra brain in. One that works. Mister Rook will want to talk to us all individually. Don't stonewall him otherwise there's no point. Ma?"

Ma looked at him and nodded, reluctantly. Her dislike of me was palpable, but not psychopathic like Tony's. I was a cuckoo in her nest and she wanted me gone.

"You could do worse than pay Harry Rembrandt a visit. Philly will tell you," said Pop.

I was left alone with Philly, who now wore jeans and a t-shirt. She puffed furiously on a cigarette, which seemed merely to feed her annoyance with the world. I'd seen her rattled and she resented it.

"I guess you always leave a window open," I said.

"How'd you know?" she asked.

"It creaks, suggesting it's been like that for a while. Also, you're a heavy smoker. It's part of the self hatred syndrome. You live in a world of smoke but you also want it gone. Presence and absence. You're probably the same with men. You want one but as soon as you get one you are sick of the sight and smell of him."

"So you're a clever dick as well as a private dick," she said, one leg swinging furiously as she perched on a chair. She was a vortex of contradictions: wanting to be in control and sexy and hard, but terrified and susceptible, her room a mix of teenage gothic trash and fluffy little girl treasures, like the doll in the toilet; any thirty year old who calls her doll Belinda has problems.

"Were you close to Danny?"

"Mum told me to say 'Yes' when you asked me that."

"And what's the truth?"

"We got on OK but truth is he was a bit stupid. Not wired out like Jimbo or weird like Tony. That's why it seemed funny that Danny got done – I mean loads of people hate Tony, join the queue, but I s'pose they're scared of him too. Maybe Danny was a bit of a sitter. Mum hates me 'cos…"

We were circling each other as much as talking. She was like a cat.

"Because what?" I asked.

"It don't matter…but grudges are like warts for Ma. You have to burn 'em off. Plus, I spoil the nest. She wanted only sons and she got me. Spent half my bleedin' childhood trying to be a boy for the old bitch. Not anymore."

This explained a lot. If you can't be a boy to get your mother's approval then experience as many men as you can to try and find out what the secret is – what is it about men that my mother so craves? I doubt if Philly would have liked this theory. For her it was all about asserting herself against Ma, not another perverse way of trying to find out how to please her.

"I was meant to be with Danny when he…"

"And why weren't you?"

"Had something else planned."

"A man?"

"There's always a man, Rooky."

"Who is Harry Rembrandt?"

"I shagged him a few times. Tony found out and went ballistic. Sent Danny round to hospitalize him. He's had a grudge ever since."

"Why was Tony upset?"

"We're like Asians. Arranged marriages. No outsiders. Rembrandt's a pillock. Don't trust anything he says."

"And why didn't Tony do his own dirty work?"

"Said it was time Danny showed he had Steele balls. It's a wotsit. Steele."

"Pun. Very funny. That psycho silhouette in the bathroom. Spooky," I said.

"Yeh, but Georgie did it. Just before he died. I'm sort of superstitious about it."

"He died in a car accident?"

"Crashed. Caught fire. Bloody gruesome. That's him."

I looked at a photograph of dead brother Georgie: a smiling, tall man in his mid thirties, wearing a curiously old fashioned suit – wide lapels and baggy trousers.

"Loved that whistle. And this was Ma when she was a girl," said Philly, nodding at a younger, much slimmer Ma, who glared ferociously at the camera. "Almost human. No, I love her really," said Philly, unconsciously touching her still pink cheek where Ma slapped her.

*

I'd had enough of the Steeles for one day, and too much to think about. I got in my car and after ten minutes realised I was being followed. A blue Mercedes. The sun visor was down so I couldn't see who was driving. I tried changing speeds and the Merc followed suit. The driver knew that I knew, but he, or she, wasn't bothered. They wanted me to know I was being followed. Perhaps it was someone from the Steele faction and they wanted me to know they were watching to see I did my job properly. It could have been Tony himself, looking for an opportunity to inch me off the road. In a single file country lane I simply stopped and waited. The Merc stopped, then a few minutes later reversed and was gone. I saw only the first two digits on the registration plate – SB.

I drove on then pulled into a lay by and rang Lizzie. I just wanted to hear her voice to know that she really exists. I also wanted to know if Cass had spoken to her. Someone else answered, not bastard destined for hell and mutilation David (now isn't that mature?) but Sadie, a harpy pseudo feminist with legs like umbrellas. I could hear screaming and a lot of bad drumming in the background.

"It's Paul. What's going on there? Has Lizzie started an abattoir in the living room?"

"We're having a Coming Home to Your Anger workshop with Rupert," she said, relishing my misery at the thought of a lot of New Age robots ruining my carpet with barefoot dancing and thumbing through my CD collection. "He studied with a Hawaiian Kahuna Spiritual teacher," she added unnecessarily.

Sadie and I have a love hate relationship. She loves herself and I hate her. She'd been trying to drag Lizzie into a world of man-hating bitterness for years. I have been maligned as a lost cause and a manipulative prick more times than I can remember. Nothing more distasteful than an enemy who is occasionally spot on and a large part of my distaste for her is that she is infuriatingly right about the darkness she sees in me.

"Is Cass there?" I asked. She wasn't. Good. That probably meant she was at my place.

"Lizzie's still wondering when you'll collect your stuff," said Sadie, relishing the barb. She suspects, and is right, that the reason I leave my stuff at what was our marital home is that I can't bear to take it. It would be a final admission that it's over, that I am no longer there. At least now, when David is slipping into my bed he knows those are my books on the shelves, my lamp he's switching off, my wife he's fucking. Does this make it easier? Of course not. It isn't meant to.

Chapter V

'All is riddle, and the key to a riddle is another riddle.'

Emerson

Cass was on the sofa, which also doubled as her bed, chewing her nails and pretending to read a book. Her eyes were not moving so she clearly wasn't reading. You need to know about Cass. She suffers from being the fulcrum between Lizzie and me. Although she's nineteen she still harbours illusions about perfection, and she wants her parents together again as doting doves to her wayward tempests, a beautiful leash of indulgence which she can strain against and test, in all her angst and bewilderment, but ultimately be reined in by – to love and safety. Now it was spoilt and she had to grow up and see the world for the contradictory, shitty mess it was, and that the life of the heart was a thorny, broken one. She didn't blame herself, though that might come, but seesawed between anger and confusion. I had gone, in her eyes, from being mere eccentric to a dangerous and irresponsible man-child. We constantly invent versions of others to suit our own fears and longings. Sometimes they even turn out to be true. Now that the family unit had imploded, it was as if scales were falling from Cass's eyes and she was seeing things and people for the first time – an alarming experience. Hopefully the full bleak picture will never reveal itself to her. Without some illusions life is impossible.

I had rented a horrible one bedroom apartment – deliberately in order to rub my own face in the awfulness of separation. It's called masochism. The lack of space meant it was impossible to avoid confrontations, even for someone as practiced as me.

"We could've got killed," she said without looking up.

"But we didn't. Cass, why the hell did you follow me?"

"Because I wanted to know. You're so secretive." She sounded like Lizzie.

"Research. I wanted to talk to them for...a book."

"You're lying."

"Of course I am, but how can we have a proper, honest, conversation if you keep insisting on the truth? It's impractical." I said. "The truth does nothing but harm."

She threw the book down. It was a decent copy of Heidegger. I hoped the spine wasn't damaged. She stood and faced me, close, eyes wide. It's what people do when they like to imagine themselves forcing the moment to a crisis.

"Please, dad. Don't play games. Just tell me."

Against instinct and better judgement, I told her enough of the truth to stop her looking at me like that. She'd probably already googled the Steeles and knew enough to realise this was serious. I said I did private investigative work, usually for people who didn't want the police involved. Desperate people. Ruthless people. Dangerous people. Her mouth opened and she gaped like a drowning person. She fell on me, arms around my neck. I hadn't expected tears so quickly. I held her. She was trembling. No. Jesus, she was giggling. She looked up at me with that heart melting grin.

"Dad, that is so cool," she said as if I was a rock star.

"You can never tell your mother," I said.

"Why on earth would I...you mean she doesn't know?"

"No. I mean, not as such, not the actual...she may..."

Cass whooped with joy. "I won't say a word to anyone. Ever. But one thing," she said.

My heart pulped into a ball. I knew what was coming next.

"The answer is no, Cass. Suppose something happened to you? You cannot be involved. Definitely not."

Half an hour later over a Chinese takeaway we'd reached a compromise. I'd tell her about my investigations and we'd discuss them; she could help with any research or internet enquiries; under no circumstances would she be physically involved. In return she would not tell Lizzie or anyone else about my twilight world.

Early next morning I was just starting a magnificent dream in which I was garrotting David with a pair of Lizzie's tights, when Cass shook me awake.

"Why do you do it? This Rook Investigations thing?"

"Out of a sense of moral and civic duty," I said.

"Liar."

"I do it because I'm a bit odd." Worryingly, this seemed to make sense to her.

"What if something happens?" she asked.

"What are you talking about? It's six in the morning."

"I mean, suppose you go missing or something. I'll have to tell someone."

"All right, you can tell Grandma."

"But she's gaga. She doesn't even know what planet she's on."

"Exactly. Now let me go to sleep."

"And another thing – twenty measly quid to get to London," she said.

"But you weren't even going to London, so I gave you twenty pounds for nothing."

"It's the principle of the thing," she said.

We were all right again.

*

An hour later I was in an art gallery that sold tasteless trash to wealthy morons. I'd phoned in sick to the university. Jeremy's ulcer would start biting, which made a good start to my day. I looked at a large exhibit, nearly three metres by two, on a white gallery wall. It was called THE M25 and on it were stuck various real squashed creatures, each with a name tag: a hedgehog (Monty); squirrel (Sid); rabbit (Florence); toad (Terence); bird (Harriet). The price was £3,900. I thought the phrase 'For those with more money than sense' should be appendaged to it.

"Window shopping?"

The voice was all North Circular vowels rolling uncomfortably like jugged pebbles around the mouth. I turned to a flash character in garish clothes, slightly gone to seed, but attractive in a fleshy young George Melly way.

"If I could afford this I'd buy something else," I said.

A smile. "If you think this is bad you should see the artist. Looks like a tin of spilled paint himself. But he knows that the public is gullible. Stick something up in a gallery, tell 'em it's art, and they start fondling their credit cards."

"Should you be talking like this to a potential customer?"

"You're not a customer. I can tell."

"No. I'm doing some work for the Steele family. My name's Rook. Trying to find out who killed Danny Boy."

"Alcohol is a sudden imperative."

In his office we both nursed large gins with slices of lemon. There were paintings stacked against the walls – better quality than the ones for sale. There were also framed film posters on the walls and film and art books on shelves. Harry took a large sip and relaxed.

"The Steeles. Pandora's box. Vipers' nest. A clutch of chaos. Tony's a philistine and warped beyond repair. Reads weapons magazines to relax." He whirled a finger around his head to indicate derangement. "Sexy in a perverse sort of way," he said.

"Pop and Philly said you might know something."

"Ah. I begin to see. Snakes in the grass."

"You wanted to see them hurt?"

"A loaded question. Even if I did, would I do it myself? Do I look like a gun toting gangster?"

"I didn't say Danny Boy was shot, and the manner of his death isn't public."

"It was a fucking metaphor."

"Do you drive a Mercedes?"

"Do I look that vulgar? Don't answer that. Mister Rook, it's very dangerous to be a keeper of secrets, but if I tell you I swing both ways and there is a lot of venom in the Steele family, you work it out for yourself. And now – I'm busy."

I left, my brain in overdrive. Philly had been playing me. Then I got it. Harry swings both ways. Ten seconds later I walked back in.

"You had a fling with Tony, then with his sister. Tony was furious, maybe even jealous, so he had you beaten up by Danny. Philly is still peeved because you had Tony too so she thinks it might be fun to get you in trouble again – maybe even blamed for Danny Boy's death. You have the motive because he hurt you."

"Clever boy."

"You think Tony killed Danny, don't you? But why?"

"Go a-way," Harry said, then looked at me, "and be very careful. It's a chamber of horrors."

As I got out on the street I got a message on my phone: **The Steele family is a sleeping viper. I'm close.** I looked up and the same Mercedes was parked about a hundred metres away. I ran towards it but it sped away. All these snake references – four in less than five minutes – coincidence or telling me something? One of the things about snakes is that you don't hear them coming. I could feel that familiar tickle of excitement. Someone was watching me. Did they want to give me information or pain? I looked in my rear view mirror as I got in my old Saab and I was smiling. There is definitely something wrong with me.

Chapter VI

'An interval of meditation, serious and grateful, was the best corrective of everything dangerous.'

Jane Austen

It was time to regroup, think, and plan my next move, but I was interrupted by another Jeremy debacle. He had complained to the Registrar that I was dangerously close to propagating racism. I was duly summoned. In a ludicrously politically correct world stupidity rises like froth on beer. The Registrar, a plump man who sweats profusely, produced a handout I had given to students as evidence of my crime. The handout contained terms of racial abuse and was part of a lecture I gave showing that one of the most powerful weapons in any act of political control is language. Words are weapons. Call someone a filthy yid and they cease to be a Jewish person. It's obvious stuff but we need to remind ourselves of the obvious, of what we say and how we say it. The Registrar listened gravely and agreed, but said we need to be careful in difficult times when student numbers were down and we live in a multi racial community. I thanked him for his time and sound advice.

Leaving his office I decided to take the next step on the road to Jeremy's breakdown. It would also cheer me up for the work ahead. You might ask: what possible pleasure can you gain from destroying someone else's mental health? The answer is simple: a great deal. Especially when they are determined to make life hell for you. As luck would have it I encountered Jeremy as I entered the Department. He looked at me smugly, hoping for the worst.

"Ah, Jeremy. Just been to see the Registrar. He's very interested in the language stuff I've been doing. Think there might even be a promotion in the air. Thanks for putting me on his radar," I said.

He didn't believe me, but he was seriously irked. He told a cleaner, an elderly woman called Dot who often chilled my chablis for me before a seminar, to get out of the way. Anyone who cares about wine deserves respect, but at least it showed the man was seriously unravelling. I went to my office and sent him an email saying that I'd noticed the unsolicited amount of attention he'd been paying me, albeit via complaints, and that if this was some sort of perverse homosexual attraction then, despite being liberal, I was not that way inclined myself and hoped this would not distress him.

On my way out he came thundering along the corridor: he'd obviously read the email.

"Doctor Rook!" he shouted.

I walked on.

A mature female student looked up from the study area and said "Excuse me, do you mind?" and made a shhh gesture.

Jeremy's fury turned on her.

"Don't shh me, you cretinous dwarf. He is an arrogant bastard and I am going to destroy him."

Now I turned. Jeremy blanched as the full horror of what he had just done overwhelmed him. He tried to bluster an apology but this mini meltdown was now blissfully public, as was the threat against me. I approached the now tearful mature student and said in my best patronising tone: "He's under a lot of pressure, poor man. As long as he remembers to take his medication I'm sure it won't happen again, will it, Jeremy?" He stood there, one eye twitching, bloodless, wanting the ground to open up and gulp him down.

Perhaps you wonder why Jeremy hates me so much. It isn't complicated. I'm not a likeable person. I do not genuflect to him. I never attend meetings, which he loves to the point of addiction. His career has, at best, been unmemorable, and he needs to blame someone for that, and I came along at the right time. He once heard me on the phone to Lizzie during which I described my Head of Department as a neutered stick insect.

My next stop was with the Staff Counsellor, a well meaning woman called Gwen sporting a faint moustache and a poster above her Mac that said "EVERYTHING IS POSSIBLE". Everything except the odd shave, apparently. I smiled and told her how concerned I was about my Head of Department, a dear colleague, who had started behaving peculiarly. Gwen crossed her legs and leaned forward, furrowing her brow to create the illusion of thought, one hand cupping her spatula chin.

"Everything you say here is in the utmost confidence."

This lie gave me the right opening. I said Jeremy seemed to be having bizarre fantasies about me in which I was both demonized yet paradoxically an object of desire. His behaviour had become aggressive and obsessive, and only minutes earlier he had terrified a student with a rant triggered merely by seeing me. Gwen nodded sagely, uncrossed her legs, thought better of it and crossed them again. I crossed mine, then uncrossed and re-crossed them to create a symmetry. There was definitely a leg subtext here. Gwen nodded sympathetically and suggested that I don't come to work for a few days to see if that calmed Jeremy a little. This was even better than I'd hoped for – Jeremy deeper in the mire and even more time off work. She said she would give the matter a lot of thought and contact me.

I left feeling I'd achieved something. The fun was over. There is something else I should tell you. I've not been entirely honest. It isn't just pleasure and revenge; this manipulation of Jeremy is also useful. It involves thinking outside the box, making things happen, creating a false narrative and then making it seem credible. It's the sort of thing I have to do in my real work – creating multiple possible stories and explanations and behaving as if each were true, to see how they hold up, and to see who might be fooling who. Proper crime investigation is a thought experiment. The Jeremy debacle is like a short workout in the gym before the big fight. I know it's unorthodox, even perverse, but it's how I do things. There is also the possibility that I'll be rumbled and it all goes horribly jerky and I enjoy that tease.

There were three things I had to consider, possibly related. Who owned the Mercedes and what did they want from me? Who was in Philly's room trying to scare the soap out of her? Who killed Danny Boy?

At home I got to work and gave Cass an extension on her Nietzsche essay so she could help. I started trawling through the Steele business interests to see if anything anomalous had happened recently that might suggest a lead. Their business profile gave them the status of the royal family, which is how Tony liked to view them anyway: connections with three High St banks; Pop on the board of over thirty companies covering transport, investment, retail, building. They'd invested in several Hollywood film companies, which was probably a money laundering or tax write off scam. Trust funds. Overseas currency trading. Huge contributions to charities. Whoever said crime doesn't pay got it very wrong.

I'd told Cass to nose about the Steele website, which was ostensibly about the family but in fact mostly a narcissistic mirror for Tony himself. I looked at her hunched over her laptop in a Save the

Badger t-shirt, a scarlet feather dangling from an earring as if her head was involved in some bizarre poultry experiment, her quick fingers playing the keyboard, eating salt and vinegar Pringles, and my heart bunched like a frightened animal. Whatever I am, friend or foe, at least she knows me. Her father has shape and substance. He may be a nightmare, but he's there. She looked up.

"Come see," she said.

Plenty of photographs of Tony getting into an Aston Martin, getting out of Aston Martin, looking at an Aston Martin, all a paean to self love and tireless self promotion. A studio photograph of Tony stared at us. Photographs of other family members, but none of Georgie.

"Eyes like dead bugs," I said.

"Good looking in an oily, predatory sort of way, but too much in love with himself to be shaggable," said Cass. My daughter never ceased to shock me. A section called STEELE VIEWS showed the family as a deeply conservative and moral force:

ROYALTY: TONY the BLADE says "Loyalty to the Queen is important. There should be more respect for her, especially among children. If they don't respect the Queen, how can we expect them to respect other adults?"

HEALTH: POP STEELE thinks it's a disgrace that people can't get operations when they need them. There should be no waiting lists.

EDUCATION: MOTHER thinks all children should be taught how to look after themselves, and that teachers should be strong minded people who can keep control in the classrooms.

Vox populi. Model citizens. Strong views but nothing radical, or criminal. And complete crap, of course. There was also a tweeting scroll that was updated every few seconds:

The Steeles rule. I want to join the family one day. John, Birmingham.

Steeles are the best thing that's happened to this country in a long time. They got pride. They sort their own. Ainsley, Bridgenorth.

Honour Tony the BLADE. "Big Boy" Nelson, Avon.

I seen Jimbo and Tony in a pub once. everyone rispects them. much more than judges and polise and gay polyticians. Jason, London.

The Steeles are like the mob and La Cosa Nostra - they have a code and they don't let no FBI or cops or no one mess with them - nice one - we heard about them over here in Chicago even - Jam, an American brother, USA.

I want to marry Tony the BLADE when I grow up. Melanie, Digbeth.

The Steeles are EXCELLENT! They's AWESOME! Steeles mean RESPECT! Longlegs John, Co. Durham.

Like Mafia, Steeles are blood and brains of the country. Benito, Harpenden.

Mad Frankie Fraser, Ronnie and Reg, Capone, Bugs Malone, Luciano, Tony the Blade. The Great Tradition. Stefano, Milan.

Steeles - pleese tell me hows I can get started. Jimmy the Break, Liverpool.

There is only honour in crime. Steeles will live forever. Alex, London.

As an indicator of the status of the Steeles in the popular mind it was scarily impressive. It also meant they were prey not only to criminal enemies, but to the violent fantasies of every fruitcake, dement, head boomer, nutter, whacko, cretin, crank, meshuggeneh and maniac in the land. The website was an invitation to any March hare with delusions of immortality to take a pot at them. It made my job almost impossible. The only way forward was backwards. Back to the family. Start at the epicentre. Concentric circles.

"They really are a law unto themselves, the Steeles, aren't they? And by drawing you in you become part of that." Cass said.

"Yup." I knew where this was going.

"Because if you do find out who killed their son, they won't go to the police."

"Nope."

"They'll deal with him, or her, themselves."

"A possibility."

"They might torture them and..."

"Cass. Consider Natural Law. If someone in your family is killed, Locke says that according to Natural Law, you have a right to kill the murderer, but where a legal system exists, you lose that right and the State takes over as avenging host. You could say that the Steele family simply cuts out the middle man: the State."

"I might use that as the opening paragraph of my essay," she said.

"Good. But the implications need a lot of unpicking. And add that Nietzsche suggests that society takes a greater delight in punishment than most criminals do."

I knew Cass would also be peeved at not coming. She was.

"But what am I supposed to do?" she asked.

"Your essay. Think how embarrassing it will be for me if I have to fail my own daughter."

"You won't. I'll get into your computer and give myself a 2:1. But I can't study all evening."

"Why don't you get a boyfriend?" I asked.

"I want a life, not some nobhead with pimples and agitated nadgers fiddling with my chest then spewing lager all over me."

"Cass, you're just an old fashioned romantic. And what the hell are nadgers?"

"Balls."

"Right. Don't stay up too late," I said.

"And I'm still appalled – twenty measly quid to get to London," she said, trying to delay my going.

"But as it was a subterfuge and you didn't really go you can give it back to me," I said.

"Cheapskate," she said and threw a cushion at me as I left. We were all right again.

*

An hour later I pulled up outside the castle. As I got out of my car the world seemed to explode and I was thrown off my feet. The sky reeled and my first thought was: *I might be dead. Supposing I've got it all wrong and there is some sort of awful unwashed God? I'll have a lot of explaining to do.*

Chapter VII

'How everyone's shadow, his gloomy travelling companion stands behind him!'
Nietzsche

I wasn't dead.

"Still slouching towards Bethlehem or Armageddon," I muttered as Philly helped me up. She looked at me as if my brains had dribbled from my ears, then shepherded me to the house. Already half a dozen besuited men were foam spraying the fire that was once Tony's beloved Aston Martin, now a melting metal inferno with great coughs of blue black smoke above it. The heat from it was palpable, so thick you could taste it. I could see why flames and fire appealed so much to fundamentalists: the screaming, pitiless force of it. My own car had shielded me from the blast but even so my balance was off and my left ear throbbed. I realised my hands were shaking uncontrollably. I have to say I enjoyed the sensation – I'd been a few metres and five seconds away from having half my body blown away. It was terrible, it was wonderful. God, there is something seriously wrong with me. The world is always gloriously full of danger if you are a coward, like me. The adrenalin started to pump; I could feel it coil in the pit of my stomach like a snake, then creep up my spine. I needed to sit down. I needed a drink. The Romantics loved flirting with death: "Half in love with easeful death." You feel the brush of the Reaper's wings and it excites; it is like illicit love with a woman while her husband sleeps next to your entwined bodies. So why don't I find it exciting that David fucks my soon to be ex-wife? It is because I find it seedy, and the thought of killing him is much more exciting. In sex and death the latter wins hands down every time. It is so final and doesn't come back like an itch to drive you mad every day. Tony pushed past me, his face a visor of pure fuck off malice. Someone would pay, I had no doubt. I hoped he didn't own a cat. No, he was too selfish to waste precious self-love on an animal.

In the room where Jimbo first interviewed me I sat down and Philly handed me a large scotch. She registered the trembling hand that took it. I looked out of the window at the blasted car. Tony was screaming at one of the men trying to douse the flames. I doubted if the fire brigade would be called or the police notified. Everything would be dealt with in-house, as usual. This is a moment when people say it is like being in a film; we are so saturated with moving images we can barely conceive of reality. But the thought brought with it a notion, something grey and half formed in the shadows. Film.

Philly was incongruously dressed in a black two piece suit. She smiled and lit a Marlborough.

"Danny Boy's funeral. And somebody tries to send Tony sky high to join him," she said. I wondered if that was true. Maybe it was more a warning. Someone showing how close they could get.

An internal phone buzzed and she indicated with a look up that it was Pop and I needed to report to him. Jimbo came in, also in a dark suit. He looked even more twitchy than before. I guess your brother murdered, a car exploding at your house, and being part of an imploding crime family might create a little stress.

"I've talked to Harry. I know about the little love triangle," I said.

"Tony don't like it put about he's a bender. I'd be very careful if I was you," said Jimbo.

"I will. Did Tony have anything to gain from Danny Boy's death?" I asked.

"No," said Jimbo, while his eyes said 'Yes. But what?'

I was led up to Pop's room. He was carefully adjusting his black tie while the shipping forecast consoled quietly: "High 200 miles west of Fitzroy 1036 slow moving, intensifying 1038 by 0600 tomorrow. Low Baltic 1008 expected Skagerrak 1007 by same time." I really was beginning to see the point of it. A calm voice in a storm, the illusion of order, the power of statistics. Behind Pop Ma was all in black, her mouth an incongruous gash of pillar box red. She reminded me of a prison warder or a Gestapo executioner.

"Mister Rook. You need to know this, if only to get it out of the way. Five years ago I told Tony I'd changed my will. Even though he was the eldest I decided to leave Georgie in charge."

"So Tony hated Georgie?"

"You humiliated the boy is what you did," said Ma, before my question could be answered. The bile rose in her like a lanced boil. Perhaps the explosion had loosed the family hinges and something useful would crawl out. Pop looked at Ma. "Moderate to poor, becoming cyclonic is what you are. What I do, I do for the sake of the family," said Pop. This further ignited Ma, who seemed to completely forget I was there. I've often noticed that if you keep still and listen intently you start to become invisible. It's useful. She swelled, red lips slick with violence.

"The family! Who do you think made this family? I bloody did. Wiped the noses and arses, kept everything together while you, bloody Champagne Charlie, was all cigars and tarts. You pissed away a fortune while I stayed up at night doing the bloody accounts. Bloody Essex playboy."

Pop turned to me.

"I apologise, Mister Rook. My dear wife has a limited education, as you can tell from the sewage pouring from the Dartford tunnel some call a mouth."

"You never treated Tone right. Always calling him a Nance even when he was a kid, making him look small to his brothers. No wonder he hated them," Ma said, getting up to full steam. "Your own son. Leaving me to patch it all up while you was off with some tart."

"Mother. Did it ever occur to you why I went off? You never wanted me. You never enjoyed it."

"I gave you five bloody kids is what I did. What more did you want?"

"A bit of ordinary love. For you to want me like I wanted you. And you never did. Did you?"

Ma's lip trembled, curled, then set. It said more than she ever could. She left. Pop passed a liver spotted hand through his thin, exhausted salt and pepper hair. He looked at me. He knew that I knew: that he let me witness these skeletons leaping from the family vault because it might help in finding his son's killer.

"It's important you know about Tony but I don't think he murdered his brother, for the simple reason I would find out and then I'd finish him. I may be an old cripple but I still put the wind up him and he can't bear it," said Pop. "And now p'raps you'd do me the honour of joining us at my son's funeral. You can't go looking like a bloody Big Issue seller, so you can wear one of Danny Boy's whistles."

Chapter VIII

'Why is it that we rejoice at a birth and grieve at a funeral? It is because we are not the person involved.'
Mark Twain

An hour later I stood in a chilly crematorium with the foremost criminal family in South England, wearing a dead gangster's suit and wondering what was still in this Pandora's box. Even the funeral was a familial bed of nails. Ma had wanted Danny cremated but Pop insisted on burial – so we stood outside in the chill of a grey English spring, the three remaining Steele children, the parents and me.

The priest began as the coffin was lowered: "Jesus said to his disciples: 'Do not let your hearts be troubled. Believe in God, believe also in me...'" and here Tony looked at his mobile phone and blanched. Pop, facing him across the yawning gap where the coffin lay in its clay bed, saw this too... "In my Father's house there are many dwelling places. If it were not so, would I have told you that I go to prepare a place for you?..." the air thickened as Pop chugged around the grave in his electric wheelchair. Philly stared down at the coffin, Jimbo looked at me, and Ma's mouth set in a thin streak of foreboding. The priest looked worried. "'And if I go and prepare a place for you, I will come again and will take you to myself, so that where I am, there you may be also.'" Pop arrived and held out his hand and like a recalcitrant and furious schoolboy Tony took the mobile phone from his pocket and gave it to Pop. "'And you know the way to the place where I am going.' Thomas said to him, 'Lord, we do not know where you are going. How can we know the way?' Jesus said to him, 'I am the way, and the truth, and the life. No one comes to the Father except through me.'" Pop suddenly reached up from his chair and hit Tony across the cheek. For a sick old man it was a hell of a slap and Tony reeled as the smack hit the air and resounded. The

Priest looked stunned and dropped his Prayer Book, which landed with a wet plop on the coffin way below. Philly walked away, lighting a Benson's; Jimbo shuffled, looked at the dead ground and half smiled; Ma looked daggers at Pop; Tony gaped at his father with the fearful repressed hatred of the buried child in him, fear masked as braggadocio, grabbed his phone back, turned on his heels and walked away. The funeral was over.

Pop's look beckoned me. The Priest scrambled down into the grave to retrieve his prayer book. I leaned down to Pop.

"Stupid sod's done something. You won't catch 'im because he drives like a mad Arab, but my bet is if you go to the factory it'll be there, whatever it is. Crabham Business Park, last on the left. The factory is Tony's responsibility," Pop said, and wrote down a code number and gave it to me. "For the security gate."

"What did the text say?" I asked.

"From some slag in the IFM. Said they know he done it and they'd take us down one by one unless he puts it right. You need to find out what 'it' is."

The factory is a warehouse where the Steeles kept a lot of goods for one of their export businesses. Tony was MD, though I doubt he spent much time poring over Excel sheets. The IFM gang, or Innit For Money, was a cartel of dealers, pushers, stealers and wheelers who got lucky with a multimillion crack heist and escalated from being petty bit criminals to players on a bigger scale, taking some of the Steele street trade. Pop wasn't worried because his vast legitimate business interests meant he could play the long game, but Tony's inflammatory ego couldn't bear the rivalry. He hated them and they knew it. Perhaps he suspected they were behind Danny's killing and had done something in revenge, or to get their attention.

"Tell 'im that if he does anything more stupid than usual, he's out. He gets nothing from me. Nothing from any of our interests."

I was dismissed. As I got in my car Philly appeared. She lit a cigarette with the one she was about to stub out. She was danger on legs.

"Most people tell me I smoke too much," she said.

"Most people are morons," I said.

"That was a farce," she said, looking back at the grave.

"Let's hope so, because a farce has a beginning, middle and end, and I'd like to see this through."

She started to walk away. I called out. "Philly! Why does Ma hate you so much?"

It took her by surprise.

"Night Georgie died I was meant to be with him but I was…otherwise engaged. Ma felt if I'd been there he wouldn't have got so off his face. She's never forgiven me."

"Have you forgiven yourself?"

"I am not my brother's keeper. He was a grown man."

She looked as if she wanted to say something else, but bit her lip and walked away. As I drove off I thought of the Steeles as a drama, a soap opera, or a

B movie. I decided the latter was most apposite. Bad film. Then it hit me again. How could I have not seen it before? A theme was emerging. I felt excited but it would have to wait. Now I had to go to the factory and see what dark little secrets Tony was keeping. First the unknown, then the paperwork.

Twenty minutes later I turned into a down at heel business park, full of rusted lockups and warehouses full of trash from Asian sweat shops. Anyone who thinks that crime is glamorous should follow me on one of these little soirees. There is a lot of grime and shit in the shadows. I saw the factory at the bottom of a cul de sac and parked my car a few hundred metres away. I walked down hugging the walls of empty businesses and warehouses. England was having its own funeral – a manufacturing one, after a slow and drugged death. We'd gone from being a nation of shopkeepers to a nation of dossers and consultants, hooked on bad TV and mindless celebrity culture. I hated celebrities, especially when they tell everyone else what to do with their money. In my revolution the intellectuals and decent plumbers would be rewarded and celebrities and bastards who fuck my soon to be ex-wife would be put against the wall. As I approached the factory I was aware of multiple cameras. I'd probably already been seen. Perhaps he was watching me now. He would be very angry – the car, the humiliation, perhaps it had flipped him and this was a bad time to follow him. What might he do? Tony's Merc, subbing for the dead Aston, was parked inside. Fences four metres high were topped with razor wire, and there was a zapped skull and cross warning about the fences being electrified, which I guess might be illegal, but who is going to prosecute the Steeles?

I walked around the perimeter to the back gate, punched in the code and entered the compound. There were a few deserted portakabin offices and a single storey warehouse the size of an airplane hangar in the centre. The front door wasn't locked, which worried me, as it probably meant I was expected. I entered. Overhead strobe lights buzzed their cicada songs over row upon row of shelves stacked with junk of every description: plastic furniture; tinned food; home decorating; cleaning materials. It was like Christmas Day in Poundland. Most of the stuff had dust on it. I knew it was there to create the illusion of sales as a front for drug or gambling money. There would be a team of accountants creating false accounts every year to suggest this was a hive of activity. What was Tony's dirty little secret here? I stopped and listened carefully. Beneath the hum there was something else. A stifled whimper. Something human, muffled, pathetic. I walked down one of the aisles to the other end of the building. There were four doors, presumably to inner offices or stores. There it was. The faint whine of human suffering. I opened the door and caught my breath at the sight of her.

Chapter IX

'I know of no book which has been a source of brutality and sadistic conduct, both public and private, that can compare with the Bible.'
James Paget

A small anonymous room with a single naked bulb. A young woman in her twenties, perhaps Eastern European, was seated at a card table, her hands strapped into a guillotine device like miniature old fashioned stocks on the table before her; each finger splayed into a separate hole, only the thumbs free. If the blade dropped she'd lose all her fingers. She was terrified almost witless, her eyes saucered with fear, eye make up streaked, her face wet with tears, sweat and snot. A gag meant she could only whimper.

"It's all right," I said, which was stupid as it was anything but all right, but never underestimate the power of platitudes. I took off the gag and she sobbed out a lungful of air then sucked in a fresh one.

"Please, please..." she said.

"It's OK. I'm going to get you out," I said.

I tried to undo the straps but they were buckled and locked. I took some paper towels from a sink, folded them and wedged them beneath the blade so even if it dropped she would be OK. The blade could be dropped by a small lever at the side so I made sure it was secure too. I looked around for a screwdriver – if I couldn't get her out of it I thought I could dismantle it. How long had she been like this?

"What's your name?" I asked.

She looked at me then her eyes glistened wetly and I knew Tony was behind me.

"Rosika. Rosika Filipov. What's it to you, Sherlock? What the fuck is it to a little weasel like you?" he said.

In the dim light he was all shadow and mad crocodile eyes. He was pale, restless, always with a slight sheen on his skin, as if something inside manufactures oil. He looks at the girl and smiles, then sniffs the air for the scent of enemies, plotters and sometimes it seems to him they are everywhere. His nemesis is a yellow vapour creeping along the window pane, slithering in through the finest crack and transubstantiating into loaded flesh and blood – the stuff of a killer in the night. This is why he can never rest. This is why he commits these atrocities. This is why he strikes first, even blindly, at everything. Especially me. He suspects I suspect him of killing his brother. Perhaps he kidnapped this girl just to prove he didn't, or perhaps it's a smokescreen to shift accusing eyes away. Either way he wants to hit me.

The girl gasped for breath. Filipov was a family name high up in the IFM gang. If Tony seriously thought they had something to do with the murder of Danny Boy and that abducting one of the daughters would provide leverage, it was stupid, but Tony's forte was not careful thought. He would also enjoy it, which is probably the main reason he did it. I could see his fist clench knuckle white. He was very angry.

"Before you hit me think of what Seneca said," I said.

He gave me a 'what the fuck' look.

"He said that anger is temporary madness. A brief tragic insanity. And it will kill you. Let me tell you what happens. Someone says something to you, or they look at you disrespectfully, or you're in a restaurant and the waiter doesn't come quickly enough, a hundred small incidents a day, and that little bubble starts to build inside you. Little red bubble. Mister Angry. He gets bigger and bigger until his breath fills your head and the only thing that will do is to hit someone. But what's really happened? Seneca says it's simply a failure of logic, of reasoning."

Tony was looking at me curiously, as if I was a creature from another planet. Perhaps I'd hooked him.

"You see. The problem is you have dangerously optimistic notions about what the world and other people are like. You expect the world to run like clockwork, you expect people to do what you want. All you need to do is lower your expectations, then you won't get so angry, and life will be better. Less optimism means less anger."

I read Tony's look of stunned incredulity as a sign that somehow I'd reached him, burrowed into that nettlebed of rage and hatred and said something that would get me out of here unharmed, preferably with the girl. I'd struck a blow for the power of logic. That's when he hit me. There really were stars. Tracers of green light. I was on the floor, I knew that because I was looking at the ceiling, even though it was undulating. I tried to say something but all that came out was "eughh." My legs had clearly dissolved to rubber because they refused to help me get up. My cheek felt as if a steam iron had been held to it. So much for logic. I'd always had my doubts about Seneca. Too simple. Reductive.

I struggled to my feet as Tony was removing the paper towels and resetting the guillotine.

"I've told 'em they get one finger at a time until they tell us who killed Danny Boy," said Tony. "And now they've torched my car I might do it anyway, just for the crack. That's what the Book says, ain't it? An eye for an eye."

"You're right that the Bible is a handbook for sadists, but consider two things. One, Pop says if you do anything to endanger the family he'll cut you out of everything, and you know he means it," I said, my wits slowly returning.

"And the second thing?"

"It wasn't the IFM that blew your car."

This got his attention. I could see the wheels spinning. If I waited long enough they might even stop and he'd ask how I knew.

"How'd you know?" he asked.

"Think about it. The security at the castle is state of the art second to none. There was no break in, yet the explosive was planted inside, right next to the house."

"So...?"

"So it was an inside job. Somebody planted it who was already there. And we still don't know if it's related to Danny's death. It might be, but it might be someone who's got it in for you, or who was paid to do it."

"Maybe by the IFM."

"But they know you've got their girl. Kill you and how would they know where she was? She could die before they got to her."

I'd planted enough doubts. He looked at the girl's frightened, pleading eyes, then at me.

"If I let her go, they'll still want me for taking her in the first place. It's a sign of weakness."

"It's a sign of strength. You know it wasn't them who torched your car, so you back off. It's a truce."

"I still think they wasted Danny Boy."

"If they did, I'll find out. But you won't achieve anything like this. You'll just start a war that no one will win."

He stood for an eternity, looking at the girl. Then the mist descended and he picked up a chair and smashed it against the wall. The small boy in him wanted to cry, the undeveloped man wanted to kill something. He hissed through his teeth, then took a silver key from his pocket and tossed it to me.

"Close the door when you leave," he said, then held my shoulders tight. I closed my eyes, thinking he was going to head-butt me, but he gave me a hard wet kiss on the mouth, looked at me, snarled "I fucking hate you," and walked out. His retreating footsteps had the chill of death as I unlocked the girl and walked her out to my car. I drove her to a cab rank.

"Make sure your family knows Tony Steele let you go voluntarily. I know you hate him but if you inflame things the chances are people you love will get killed too."

She nodded and breathed a thank you, and was gone. I felt like Sir Galahad and hated it. It didn't fit. I needed to create a bit of chaos to feel like myself again.

Chapter X

'I fear the day technology will surpass our human interaction. The world will have a generation of idiots.'

Albert Einstein

I can hack. I'm very good at it. I shouldn't be because I hate machines. They smell me coming and usually conspire against me. Drink dispensers go dry; cash dispensers chew up my card; rail ticket machines send me to appalling places: but I think my desire to go to forbidden zones, be where I should not be, is an engine of transgression that permits me the technological ability to invade other people's lives precisely at times and places they hope to preserve in secrecy. The incident with Tony and the girl had rattled me. I also needed to explore the idea I'd had about the murder of Danny Boy Steele. First, though, I needed to let off a little steam. I know Jeremy is an easy target but I was saving the bigger fish of David and Lizzie for the end of the week.

I regularly hack into Gwen the Counsellor's computer. I know who is having what kind of breakdown at any given moment in the University; I know everyone's fetishes and psychoses; I know who is knocking off whom and how often. These people do not interest me, but I see it as a form of cataloguing – an ordering of the psychological and emotional ruins of my dreary colleagues. Gwen is pathetically diligent and films all of her sessions, presumably so she can review the minutiae and body language of her clients. I have set my hack to record anyone connected with me, so I now have Jeremy's first painful revelations of his soul to watch over a bottle of Rioja. It is hilarious:

He sits in complete misery, his lips blanched.

JEREMY: I've been under a lot of strain.

Gwen holds up a pink cushion.

GWEN: Would you like to hit this cushion?

JEREMY: No. I very much do not want to hit that cushion.

GWEN: Jeremy, I think your anger against Dr Hawkins is a displacement activity. It's not about him at all. He's a conduit for other anxieties in your life.

JEREMY: It is completely, absolutely, unequivocally about him. It is very much about him. It is always and only about him. He is a vain, arrogant, workshy adolescent who is too clever for his own good.

GWEN: Are we accessing envy here, I wonder? Is it his cleverness you hate in particular?

JEREMY: No, it's all of him I hate. Every bit.

GWEN: And what would you like to happen to him?

JEREMY: I'd like to see him put against a wall and shot through the head. Again and again and again. And then boiled in fish oil and garotted and I'd like a very large elephant to sit on his balls.

GWEN: I'm going to make a suggestion you won't like. I want you to befriend him.

JEREMY: You must be barking mad.

GWEN: Think about it. You say he antagonises you deliberately. That he's the bane of your life. And it seems you always rise to the bait. But if you modify your behaviour, let him see that you're indifferent to insults or slights, then perhaps he'll stop doing it. Will you try it? Just ask him to have a drink after work one evening. Be friendly. Cordiality, even if it's disingenuous, is often the best means of diffusing tensions in the workplace.

JEREMY: But I hate the bastard.

GWEN: Perhaps you don't have a choice. You said it's beginning to rule your life, that the mere thought of him sends you into a murderous rage. You have to do something. Don't you?

Jeremy looks at his clenched knees in utter misery.

This cheered me up considerably. I switched off the recording on my computer. However I decided to play it from here would be entertaining. I poured another glass of wine. The fun was over. I brought up a photograph of Danny Boy's trussed body, then

I started doodling ideas and connections: the snake references; *As Time Goes By*; the bomb in the car; the Merc; the doll with pages in its mouth; the Hitchcock shower scene on Philly's shower. There was a film theme here: Danny Boy's body was trussed up like Cagney's in *Public Enemy*; the doll was like the murdered lover in *The Cook, The Thief, his Wife and Her Lover*; in *Psycho*'s shower scene the girl gets killed; Bond's Aston Martin gets blown up in *Skyfall* though no one gets killed in that scene. Perhaps Tony wasn't meant to be killed either. Philly escaped death too, but maybe that was deliberate – the important thing about the shower scene is that the killer is someone pretending to be someone else, and it sends the audience the wrong way temporarily. Is that what someone was doing here? *As Time Goes By* has always been a Death of Love scene to me. Now I had a theme – the murder of Danny Boy was part of a movie theme involving murder or attempted murder. Those murders, or murder attempts, usually involved revenge, retribution.

I needed to talk to the Steeles, but suddenly Cass was there; she had an unnerving habit of appearing at my shoulder. It must be like having a conscience. She was wearing her furrowed brow, which meant she was thinking.

"This Natural Law thing. It seems to me you can only have a legal system that punishes crime if it's based on a belief in Natural Laws. There has to be a belief system in the first place," she said.

"A belief that some things are right and some wrong precedes any legal system, and without which that system is based on nothing. The problem is – the word 'natural.' Is it natural to stone an adulteress to death? Is it natural to chop off someone's hand for stealing?"

"It's all social, isn't it? It's all made up – to protect someone's interests?"

I smiled. She was getting somewhere.

"Maybe you and Mum should talk. Why don't you ask her out?" She said from left field.

"A date? It's a bit late for that," I said, no longer smiling.

"You realise that if you find another woman, you'll start comparing her with Mum and it'll all go hopelessly wrong," she said.

"Thanks, Cass. I have to go."

"The Steeles?"

"Yes. If you want a break from your essay you can do a search for me. Killers that have a movie fetish. What sort of psychological profile? Anything really."

Her face lit up and my heart reeled.

Chapter XI

'I hate to advocate drugs, alcohol, violence, or insanity to anyone, but they've always worked for me.'

Hunter S. Thompson

Jimbo was concerned. Pale, skin like dried leaves, dilated pupils, unwashed. We were in my old Saab driving to Harry's gallery. Jimbo was a man with strange corners. On the face of it, a pampered young criminal who was seriously off the rails in terms of his drug intake; also, someone of quirky and studious interests: photography, genealogy. It was the latter that caused the problem. He'd reached back as far as 1640 in the lineage that led to the present Steele incarnation. In a sense he was the most interesting Steele, by which I mean complicated, apart from Pop.

He'd been making a map of the family tree. See the scene as I do. Tony enters and starts scoffing at it. Anything requiring sustained concentration is queer in Tony's book, and given his own innate queerness he wants to destroy it. This is a schizoid form of self-loathing, an unconscious desire to destroy himself. He hates the fact that Jimbo has interests, occupations, things that take him away from and into himself. He looks at Jimbo's tree of family networks and connections he has drawn on his Mac and he instantly wants to belittle it, or better, destroy it. Jimbo's preoccupation fails to alert him to the seething brew of malice in his brother. He points out names, photographs. Great Aunt Bet who knocked out Great Uncle Eric's teeth with one punch. Wallop. Hams like buckets. Great Great Grandma, who went bald overnight when her son Ernie got his head blown off at the Somme. And there, a cul de sac in the veined lines. 1784. Jennifer Steele. Tony sniffs a secret, an indiscretion, an anomaly. He points. Who's that?

"In the Parish register it says she was the village idiot," says Jimbo, smiling, almost affectionate for this hounded soul who would now be cosseted as having learning difficulties. It is enough to short circuit Tony. Any excuse.

"We did not come from some mad bitch!" he says, and punches the keyboard, which scrambles everything.

"That was a week's work. You need help, bro," says Jimbo.

Now Tony has a reason for flipping, which is what he wanted.

"You saying I'm a sicko or something?" and so it escalates with Tony's byzantine logic leading him to criticise me and anyone associated with me.

"I bet that ponce Harry has been saying stuff about me…I've had enough!" And off he stalks. Tony has an errand to run for Pop, which gives Jimbo time to call me. Why does he want me there, given that I inflame Tony further? I think I calm Jimbo. I'm an outsider, a reminder of life outside the Steeles.

We arrive at Harry's. He stands before the M25 piece, explaining its intricate splendours to a man in Elton John specs and a check jacket of which Coco the Clown would have been proud.

"I see it as a metaphor for the gratuitous and indifferent violence at the heart of modern culture."

Cue the mad dervishing swirl of Tony suddenly there and on Harry before any of us can react. He'd clearly done a lot of sniffing to power his juices for this, to judge by his eyes. He slams Harry's head into the M25 and many of the squashed victims fall off, then as Harry goes down Tony kicks him in the face. He takes the M25 framed canvas from the wall and smashes it over Harry's head and then he takes a small axe from his pocket and everyone tenses.

"Don't ever, ever talk about me to anyone, you shirt-lifting little queer. You dirty little animal!"

He raises the axe and then turns and starts hacking at the canvases on the wall. The man in the clown jacket slithers down the wall, his mouth open and specs askew.

"Tone! Stop!" shouts Jimbo. "Tone, get out before the police come."

This arrests Tony. He stops and looks around, spittle swinging from his mouth, vaguely surprised at the carnage, as if it is nothing to do with him. He drops the axe.

"Go!" says Jimbo.

Tony looks like a panicky schoolboy caught with his fingers in the biscuit tin. He runs out. Jimbo turns to the Coco man.

"Get lost," he says.

The man gathers what is left of his wits and dignity and leaves. Harry groans on the floor. Teeth are broken, perhaps his whole jaw, one eye closed. I try to help him up but he waves me away.

"This is you. Bastard. He'd forgotten about me until you came along. What did you do to get him like this?"

"Nothing," I say.

Jimbo was surprisingly good in this crisis. Without Pop overshadowing everyone he came into his own more.

"I'll sort an ambulance. You'll be OK, Harry. We'll pay for this. You might even be better looking with a bit of cosmetic. Don't say nothing to the old bill, but you know that."

Jimbo rang for an ambulance, then we left. It would only get complicated if we were there when people arrived. I had to go to the university and check a few things before meeting the family to tell them my current thoughts.

*

In my office I scrolled through news reports of Georgie Steele's death. I stopped at CRIMINAL DIES IN HORROR CRASH. A photograph of a burnt out car. It said **"...Fond of fast cars, drunk, he drove straight into a lamp post, the engine sparked and by the time the fire brigade was there the whole car had burnt out. Georgie Steele liked seeing his family as part of a gangster tradition. He enjoyed life in the fast lane and that is how he died. He often wore suits reminiscent of 1930s gangsters – wide lapels, double breasted, and trilby hats."** Something about the car. I zoomed in. There was a strange dent in the roof of the car above the back seat behind the driver. I printed it off. Another paper had a more gruesome photograph of the charred body in the car. I printed that too.

*

Pop was in a subdued mood. Jimbo and I gave him a slightly tame version of the gallery scene, but he probably guessed. He didn't ask where Tony was. He knew he would keep his distance for a while. *Thames, Dover Wight* …played soothingly in the background and one of Pop's hands moved as if conducting the voice in its litany of place names and warnings. His presence filled the room like a vapour. I'd told them that I was looking for someone who had both a grudge against the family, or Danny in particular, and who had a fascination with films.

"I like Disney meself. Bambi. Lady and the Tramp. Heart-warming stuff. Not all that violent gangster crap," Pop said, while Jimbo smirked in a corner and Philly stood near the window blowing out smoke. She flickered with obscure inchoate needs. Ma was perhaps in some dark corner of the house sharpening her talons.

"There's Mac," said Philly.

"That's right," said Jimbo. "He tried starting a film company but sacked everyone when they didn't do what he wanted. Nutter about films. Had his own little cinema in his gaff. His crew has to go and watch a classic movie every week. Popcorn, the lot." Jimbo looked terrible. I suspected a lot of coke had been snorted since the Harry incident to judge by the jittery eyes and wondered if Pop knew. He probably did. Jimbo was all cool assurance in the gallery and now he was a mess. Action, reaction, action, reaction; that's how he worked.

"And what has Mac got against you?"

"We edged him out of a property deal a few years back. It got nasty. Messy. Someone ended up in the foundation stones of a block of flats near Peckham," said Pop.

"A few years back. Why wait until now?" I asked.

"Slow burner. Mac don't go in for kneejerks. It'd be like him to wait," said Jimbo.

"Smart too. We'd be less likely to connect him with Danny Boy's murder," said Philly.

"What's Mac's surname?" I asked.

"Donald," said Jimbo.

"You are joking," I said.

They weren't. Philly followed me as I left. In the hall downstairs I stopped and turned.

"Are you wondering what I'm like in bed?" she asked.

"You mean when you're asleep? Inert, I imagine, with face cream and curlers." I said. This young woman was a bramble bush of insecurities and bad news.

"You know what I mean," she said.

"You don't want me. You just want to see if you can have me. If I said 'Yes' you'd switch off. You're just fed up with the men who run scared because of who you are, or those who think they might get a slice of the family dosh, and most of whom are uncultured deadheads who bore you silly within minutes of opening their mouths. You know I'm not impressed with you, which is why you're intrigued," I said.

Her cheeks pinked slightly.

"Fuck off," she said.

Princess, Queen of Words, Enchantress. She would make some poor man utterly miserable one day.

Chapter XII

'For many men that stumble at the threshold are well forewarned that danger lurks within.'

W. Shakespeare

I went back to my grubby little flat to change. Cass would be there, excited about what she'd discovered. By giving her these jobs in relation to my work I was also keeping her at a distance from it. I wondered how long it would be before she worked that out.

"Killers who say they were inspired by films usually want the notoriety that goes with the film and the character," she said as soon as I entered. "Copycat killers associate with the glitz of the original."

"So that doesn't work, given that this killer also wants to remain undiscovered," I said.

"That's where depersonalization comes in. The killer adopts the persona of a killer, a bit like being the actor, only in their own mind, and the character is a sort of reflected glory. Also, the persona puts a distance between them and the murder. They can hide behind the mask," she said.

"The mask is not something to hide behind, but to express something," I said. "So, in a sense, the mask is not pretend but a way of enacting something very real – a grudge, a psychosis," I said.

She looked crestfallen.

"If you know all this stuff, why did you ask me to do it?"

"Cass, we're just discussing it. What you did was incredibly useful. Thanks."

She perked up a little, but I knew she was suspicious. I work hard at not being known, but my own daughter had eerily accurate hunches about me sometimes. We had a Chinese takeaway and watched *No Country for Old Men*, one of our favourite comedies. One of the many things Lizzie found difficult about me was how violent films made me laugh. Luckily Cass didn't share that prejudice. I like films because even the good ones only occupy a small part of your attention and my mind can wander before the flickering, absurd images. I wondered what peculiar bits of DNA in me I had inherited from my father. It would be just my luck to find the bastard the day after he dies.

*

Mac Donald's front was a club in Mayfair called Red. Red leather and wallpaper, mirrors everywhere, cheap champagne, Armani legs and Gucci breasts: everything that would make any sane person wish for Armageddon. I had a whisky and looked at nothing in particular. He was sat in a corner with a man who looked like a psychotic chartered accountant: neat, clipped, tight mouthed, and non-descript suit. I'd prepared a scenario. It was both daring and stupid and could go horribly wrong, designed to test his reactions and give me some clue about the inner man. I could spend weeks watching him, making enquiries, or do this. There was no choice. Five minutes later psycho accountant nodded to me and I joined them.

Mac was business-like and wet eyed, good looking if you get the hots for frogs fresh from the pond, a filigree of tiny acne scars that made his cheeks look like a road map stitched from delicate lace. Armani suit. Hand stitched shoes. He didn't offer me a refill.

"So what is it?" he asked.

"Straight to the point. I like that," I said.

I opened the briefcase I'd brought especially for the occasion and took a file of property flyers I'd got from an estate agents that morning, then doctored on Photoshop with a fake banner and logo: I was now the Head of Sales for Waterside Developments, a real company name but now with a new non-existent brief. I was using the real name of Head of Sales: Clive Springer. I spread a few out. Mac looked at them in a desultory way. Psycho boy examined them as if he were a Babylonian Priest studying entrails. I was about to launch into my spiel when Mac held up his left hand while he made a call with his right. He listened then stopped the call and looked at me.

"It had better be good," he said.

"Sorry?" I asked.

"I put in a call to Waterside. They say they've no knowledge of this meeting, so I'm listening for the next thirty seconds before two of my employees appear and take you to a safe place where they will break your arms and legs and nail your tongue to a bread board."

"This is a non-protocol meeting. I thought you probably understood that…it puts me in a difficult position if you don't," I said.

"You're in a difficult position anyway. What do you mean?" Mac asked.

"We're one of the most successful property companies in London for Waterside residential and business properties. Quality end of the market. The main reason for our success is our fast track strategy. We keep a vigilant eye on mortgage defaulters and pending bankruptcies then buy at knockdown prices and sell on. The fact that we also hold the mortgages and can suddenly ask for increased repayments that we know the borrower cannot afford puts us in a very advantageous position. The paperwork needs to be in place quicker than is usual, if you get my drift, and we need a considerable cash flow ready in an instant from wealthy and successful people..." I genuflected at him, "...who understand what we are doing and who will make a considerable profit, sometimes as much as forty per cent return, in a matter of weeks. Meetings such as this don't...formally exist, if you get my drift."

I indicated the sumptuous properties on display. Psycho stood up, walked a little away and made a call.

"These will make a huge return within weeks. We have a second to none legal department so there are no awkward questions asked."

"So you set people up to bankrupt them. Sounds like it's floating very close to breaking the law," said Mac, smiling. "Who else have you approached?"

"Client confidentiality. We are very discriminating and very discreet. I can tell you a few people who have approached us but we decided to turn down. Complications. Ben Gazann the oil magnate. The Steele family. A few others."

His eyes flickered at the mention of the Steeles but nothing more.

"So why approach me?" he asked.

"You're a successful businessman. You probably have the sort of money we need short term. You probably like to make a hefty profit."

I smiled, ostensibly to myself.

"What?" he asked, looking at Psycho, who had finished his call.

"A quirky reason too. I'm a movie buff. It's a passion. I heard that you are too," I said.

Mac looked at me long and hard. "Yes, I like films. What's your bag?"

I played my most dangerous card.

"Eclectic. But my favourites would have to include Cagney's *Public Enemy* – the trussed up body still shocks after all these years; *Cook, Thief,*

Wife, Lover; *Psycho*. Not a Bond fan but I did like *Skyfall*. That Aston. Boom!"

He weighed my choices. I knew then he wasn't the killer. There was nothing on that face, no slight dilation of the irises, no change in colour, no eyebrow movement, to suggest he was. Some profilers say you can tell nothing from facial architecture or body language and it is only in speech – logical gaps, hesitations, confusion – that criminals reveal themselves. Language is the real key but everything else counts too, if you know how to read the flutter of an eyelash, the tightening of a pulse, the twirl of a finger. He was about to say something when his mobile rang with Beethoven's *Fur Elise*. He said nothing but I knew it was bad news. The air seemed to chill and my throat suddenly parched. I wished I'd ordered a treble. The call finished.

"Guess who that was?" he asked.

"Sugar Plum Fairy?" I said, feeling my goose was already in the oven and heating up.

"Clive Springer. So either he was speaking from a parallel universe or you are a con artist who's made the biggest mistake of his life."

I opened my mouth to spin a rope of lies but he put a finger to his lips.

"My colleague here, and my other colleague there…" a man the size of a small African continent appeared, "…are going to walk you out of my club and into the car park, where they will drive you to a beautiful little spot in the country, then give you a nice picnic before dropping you home."

"I believe everything up until the picnic part," I said.

I was sweating so much I could barely see. The African Continent helped me to my feet and guided me out by my elbow. Why is it, at such moments, that we don't shout and scream?

It's because Terror subdues us.

Chapter XIII

'The object of life is not to be on the side of the majority, but to escape finding oneself in the ranks of the insane.'

Marcus Aurelius

I wondered where we would go and what would happen. I would be given something to remember – hopefully no broken bones or cracked teeth. I fastened my seat belt tight, as if that would somehow protect me against these two gangsters. African Continent drove and Psycho sat stonily beside him. I thought that he probably had a clipboard with a checklist to be assiduously ticked off: *Item: one punch to kidneys. Check. Item: head butt to nose. Check. Item: nose broken. Check.* I was so scared it was like a form of paralysis. People say 'paralysed with fear' and not for the first time I thought how clichés become clichés because they capture a truth lost in repetition and over usage.

"It's all right. You can just drop me here; I'll get the bus home," I said. Inappropriate responses seem to be second nature to me. I should be pleading, begging, bribing.

Psycho registered nothing but his partner smiled in the mirror at me. I did what I do at the dentist to take my mind somewhere else; remember speeches. Hamlet seemed appropriate and I started intoning:

"To be, or not to be: that is the question:

Whether 'tis nobler in the mind to suffer

The slings and arrows of outrageous fortune,

Or to take arms against a sea of troubles,

And by opposing end them. To die: to sleep;

No more; ..."

African Continent looked at me in the mirror. He was rattled. "What the fuck are you doing? Put a fucking sock in it!" he said.

Psycho said nothing and stared ahead at the traffic as we drove past Goodge Street station towards Warren Street, then left into Maple Street.

"...and by a sleep to say we end
The heart-ache, and the thousand natural shocks
That flesh is heir to, 'tis a consummation
Devoutly to be wish'd. To die, to sleep;
To sleep: perchance to dream: aye, there's the rub;
For in that sleep of death what dreams may come,
When we have shuffled off this mortal coil,..."

In the corner of my eye I register the blue Mercedes driving at full tilt up Maple Place towards us and just have time to brace myself and put my hands over my head before it slams into the front passenger side. Psycho's head jerks and then jerks back horribly, like a broken puppet. The driver's head slams against the side glass, which cracks. The car spins, almost overturns, checks, spins again, then hits a waste bin and crunches to a halt. A pause that seems like an eternity and everything stills: dust motes; a startled pigeon; a woman drops her Sainsbury's bag; irregular grouting on a wall; an orange rolls merrily across the road and banks against the kerb. Miraculously I seem OK, apart from being even more terrified. The Merc is reversing. I try to see the registration plate but only get a DW. The driver seems to have a woollen head. He turns and is wearing a balaclava; a flash of eyes and mouth. Then he is gone. People start to gather around our car, hungry for blood, something to tell. The driver is out cold and Psycho clearly has something broken – a shoulder or arm, and is in agony. I do what any cowardly self-preservationist would do. I get out of the car, almost fall as my jelly legs seem determined to fail, then those great engines of speed – fear and adrenalin – kick in and I run faster than I have in years. There is a taxi at the traffic lights and I jump in, next to a startled woman with a Botox forehead and a Gap bag stuffed with useless goodies. "Wherever she's going is fine," I say. It has been an interesting afternoon.

What had I achieved? I had eliminated a suspect. I'd been involved in a car crash in which my mystery Merc driver saved me from a beating, or worse, but was this to protect me or save me for himself? If it was a him. It would be very unlikely that Mac could trace me. I wondered how seriously his two men were injured. Very seriously, I hoped.

As I approached my flat I knew that the Merc was the key. I decided my next move would be to do something that would make my knight errant driver appear, and try to get the number at least. Stupid of me not to have clocked it. DW. The first time I saw it the first two letters were SB. Although the car was at least ten years old the number plate was new, which meant the driver kept changing the plates. Whoever it was did not want to be found.

Even as I open the door I know. The air flurries expectantly. Cass by the window in a flutter of hopeful anxiety. Lizzie draped like satin over my one comfortable chair. Languishes for effect, strains for relaxation. Brings the scent of lavender, sex and something woody, as if she has just come from a public burning. Cat eyes. Blonde hair bobbed and shiny. She has taken up primal screaming and reiki; I know these things from Cass, whose desperate plotting is designed to create a rapprochement that can only fail. Lizzie. I love her madly. I want to strangle her. I decide to start with subtlety. An ice breaker.

"David still in bed? Not sweating his tedious corrupt politics into my Vietnamese silk bed robe, I hope?"

Cass winces. The innocent always get it in the neck. Liz stands. "I knew this was a mistake": this to Cass. *Please please try*: this a look from Cass at me. *To hell with it*: this to myself. Then Liz is gone. I can imagine her more effectively without her.

"Indian takeaway?" I ask.

At 3 am I got a call from Jimbo. The factory. Now. Tony is dead.

Chapter XIV

'I have been merely oppressed by the weariness and tedium and vanity of things lately: nothing stirs me, nothing seems worth doing or worth having done: the only thing that I strongly feel worth while would be to murder as many people as possible so as to diminish the amount of consciousness in the world. These times have to be lived through: there is nothing to be done with them.'

Bertrand Russell

Jimbo opened the door to the Factory. He looked older, haggard, perhaps full of *Am I next*? thoughts.

"What time did you find him?"

"About nine. I got an anonymous text, number withheld."

He showed me the text: **THE FACTORY. TONY. They are going to say this was a dignified revenge killing.**

"He was choked. There's screwed up paper in his mouth – a photograph of the family," I said.

Jimbo stopped, his mouth open.

"How'd you know?" he asked, genuinely impressed.

"'They are going to say this was a dignified revenge killing' is a line from Albert in *The Cook, The Thief, His Wife and Her Lover* when he murders his wife's lover the same way that Tony has now been murdered. The doll in Philly's toilet wasn't some weird one off perversion. It was a warning. A statement of intent. We're dealing with someone who has a plan."

In the same small room where the girl had been kept Tony was on the floor, mouth stuffed with crumpled paper – a copy of the same family photograph. I took it out.

"I think the message here is: stuff the family," said Jimbo. "Like a runaway car all his life."

"I suppose I should say sorry," I said.

"Don't be. He was a selfish, vicious bastard. Just one less car on the road."

I was starting to like Jimbo. No phoney sentimentality that often went with criminals. Tony's face had the purplish stains of a choke victim. There was an abrasion on his forehead. A whack on the head and then enough paper to choke him. I felt in his pockets and took his mobile phone, checked the last calls and texts he'd sent and received. Mostly trash, but the last text exchange was interesting:

?: Meet me at the Factory 6pm.
TONY: WHO IS THIS?
?: Someone close. You'll be glad you came.
TONY:WHATS YR NAME?
?: Marko.

That was the whole exchange. Suddenly a new text flashed up. The same font.

Hi Rook. You ever dance with the devil in the pale moonlight?

I looked around. The timing was too perfect. How did they know I'd have the phone at that precise moment? Was I followed? 'You ever dance with the devil in the pale moonlight?' was a line from the Joker in the 1989 *Batman*. I texted back:

ME: Is that what I'm doing now?

?: Sure. May the force be with you.

ME: Do you only ever communicate with lines from movies?

?: Yes. We all go a little mad sometimes.

ME: Norman Bates in Psycho?

?: Very good.

ME: What's all this really about?

?: You can't handle the truth. Bye for now.

That was it.

"Who's Marko?" I asked.

Jimbo frowned. "Marko was a Maltese guy that Tony was crazy about. I mean flowers and satin hearts cuckoo crazy. Then Marko disappeared."

"You mean he just left?"

"Pop made him an offer. Fifty grand to fuck off and never come back. Pop felt Tony's obsession was becoming an embarrassment to the family, and he kept taking his eye off the ball, business wise. I guess Marko preferred the dosh to Tony's dick. Or maybe he was scared Pop would change the offer to something more permanent."

"And no one heard from Marko again?"

"Nope."

"And Tony never mentioned him?"

"As if he'd never existed. Tony wasn't exactly a sentimental type. And once his pride is wounded…" He looked down at the body, "… *was* wounded, he either lashed out in revenge or rubbed people out of his thinking. No halfway house with Tony."

*

It was getting hard for me to tell red herrings from a genuine catch. Marko's surname was Dolivier. At home I made the usual checks through online address lists in Malta and the UK (though Marko could have gone anywhere and probably changed his name), then through social networks. It's amazing how people think they are still invisible, even when they use Facebook and other networks. Cass used my laptop to look up movie buff sites to see if he appeared on any. Nothing. I sat down with a glass of Famous Grouse and Cass sipped a glass of white wine. It was a nice moment. Quiet. Like most nice moments it soon got disturbed. She was staring at the laptop screen.

"Why are you your own worst enemy?" she asked.

"Because that way I'm never surprised by what other people do."

"Mum wants me to move back in with her."

"And…?"

"What do you want?"

"That's not fair," I said.

"I'm caught in the middle," she said. "And I know you hate David, but you're not exactly Mister Innocent, are you?"

I sensed a bombshell. A pause.

"I know about Annie or Fanny or whatever her name is," she said, indicating the laptop screen.

"If you've looked at my emails then you know it's Anna. It's nothing. It's over," I lied.

"So that's why she says she can't wait for Friday night at her place?"

"Cass, haughty and superior doesn't suit you."

"I just think it's a bit hypocritical for you to go on about Mum and to hate David when you've got some woman on the go too. And Mum doesn't even know about…Anna. And you play this wounded victim crap…It's deceitful. Immoral."

"Cass! Why do you want to complicate my pure unviolated hatred for David with morality and truth and nonsense like that?" I asked, irritated, my Famous Grouse mood turning to bile.

"Sometimes I can't believe my own father is a Philosopher when he talks such complete bollocks."

Lizzie was in that rising temper, the horns growing.

"But that's an excellent definition of a philosopher. Someone who talks complete bollocks," I said. "Why do you think no one ever listens to us?"

"You turn everything into a joke. As if nothing means anything."

"Maybe everything is a joke. Maybe nothing has meaning," I said, wishing I could boil my own head.

Cass stormed out and left the door singing on its hinges.

"But you mean everything to me, Cassie darling. Nothing I wouldn't do...I'm sorry," I said to the emptiness. I was taking being my own worst enemy to dizzying new depths.

Yes, I haven't been quite straight. It's an interesting legal and philosophical point, whether an omission amounts to a lie. I have a woman. Anna. Full breasted and compliant. She offered and I took. It is one of the few uncomplicated things in my life. We see each other about once a month and offer each other a night of irresponsible lust. Uncluttered with talk about the past and the future together, with its little minefields and thousand small barbs, its pillowed suspicions, hidden agendas and unconscious manoeuvrings – the stuff of serious relationships for which human beings are entirely ill equipped. We make absurd promises during the night that would never be cashed in – we knew that; it was part of the delight. Liz knew nothing about Anna. The difference was I found out about David, which gave it an epic status in our imploding lives. The difference was David mattered, whereas Anna and I had no such illusions about each other. The difference was I still loved Lizzie beyond sanity whereas when she started humping David it changed something. The fact that David was my best friend gave it a nightmare status too. If you can't see the differences then I envy you.

Luckily my self-justifying ramblings were interrupted by a text: **Meet me at 12 Geordine Gardens. 8 pm. Door will be open.** I hoped this wouldn't be another doomed complication in the Steele case. There were no movie references. Might it be Marko and, if so, what would be waiting for me?

Chapter XV

'The sentence you are reading is false. The next sentence is true. The previous sentence is false.'

The Liar Paradox

12 Geordine Gardens was a row of nondescript terraced houses. Call me an old idealist but I found them depressing and probably full of tattooed dysfunctional families with bull terriers and numerous unwanted babies, who all hated each other. It's not snobbery, but a terrible despair over the condition of England. The philistines are not merely at the gates, they are on the sofa watching SKY TV with lapfuls of lagers and fast food. The door was open, as promised. I entered and immediately the smell of fungoid damp and the untouchedness of everything told me that no one lived here.

"Hello?" I said.

Nothing. A downstairs front room the size of an egg box, curtains drawn, dust on a mottled mirror; a few steps out to a kitchen diner with a Formica table and three chairs, 1960s kitsch, old cooker, fridge, bare cupboards save for a box of teabags. Electric plastic kettle, still warm. So someone was here, or had been.

I went upstairs, listening hard. Toilet and bathroom and two bedrooms. The first one had the windows boarded up with plywood, a single mattress on the floor, a mug by the bed with something green growing in it. A wisp of noise behind me. I turned and my heart jumped.

"Ma!" I said.

She stood like a funereal troll in the doorframe, black coated, steel grey hair permed like a crusader's helmet. "Mrs. Steele to you," she said.

"So you sent the text?" I said.

"Yes." Her eyes flickered.

"How did you know I'd have Tony's phone?"

"Know more than you think," she said.

Five minutes later we made an unlikely pair in the back yard, a small concrete tip of rubbish, including an incongruous daisy growing from a cushion. I sat on a broken wooden chair and she sat on the ripped, moulding seat of an Astra, chewing on a garibaldi and sipping her thrice sugared tea, this woman who could afford to build a castle overlooking Lake Garda.

"What is this place?" I asked.

"Safe house. We 'ave a few of 'em all over. In case…in case…" she said.

"I'm sorry about Tony," I said disingenuously.

She closed her eyes against tears, took a swig of tea, a nibble of her biscuit, and was restored.

"I want you to leave off. Nuff's enough," she said.

"I can't do that. Pop…Mr Steele has employed me…"

"I'll give you five grand," she said.

"You've lost two sons. Don't you want the killer found?" I asked.

"I think whoever it is might stop if you back off."

"Why? Has someone contacted you?"

She hesitated.

"Yes. They said if you stop they will. I've lost enough," she said.

"But why will they stop? Who is it?"

"How should I bloody know? I just got a call. Telling me. Now I'm telling you. Stop," she hissed.

"I'll talk to Pop. That's all I can promise," I said.

"Ten grand," she said.

"I'm sorry."

"Please."

"I'm sorry."

She looked at me, a tight little ball of hatred and rage.

"You bloody will be if I lose any more. Now piss off," she said. I stood up. Ma hesitated. "Philly ain't got no time for me. We're like ice and fire. Seems to like you. When you go to the Castle, tell 'er to be careful."

I nodded.

Outside I waited in my car, a little down the road. Ten minutes later Ma emerged. She got in a maroon Ford that I hadn't seen at the Castle and drove away. I followed. She parked outside a Tesco Express and ten minutes later came out with two carrier bags of goodies. Something about this made no sense. I followed her car until I was sure she was going to the Castle, then left.

I puzzled things again. Two murders. An obsession with film. The Mercedes following me. Lots of snake references. I went to the University to cancel tomorrow's lectures. In my office I found a bottle of rioja in a drawer marked Current Research and poured a large one in an almost clean mug. I brought up the photographs on my computer of Georgie's death: the burnt out car with the hole in the roof and the charred body of Georgie Steele. It was difficult to tell but the car looked to me like a Mercedes. I phoned Jimbo and asked what sort of car Georgie used to drive.

"Mercs. Always Mercs. Blue ones," he said.

I asked him to send me some attachment photos of Georgie, especially the one that hung on the living room wall. He promised he would.

"What are you having for supper tonight?" I asked.

"What? Why?"

"Just tell me. It's important."

"I'm out. Philly – who knows? We don't go in for family meals – they usually end in a barney. One of the boys cooks for Pop and Ma," he said.

"And who does the shopping?"

"Jimmy. The one who cooks."

"So Ma doesn't shop for the meals? No supermarket run?"

"Ma. No. Funny that."

"What is?"

"She always used to cook when Georgie was alive, but never since. He liked her steak and kidney."

"And she stopped when he died?"

"Yes."

So why was Ma shopping? I found it hard to believe she had a secret lover unless he had Byzantine tastes in women. A knock on the door and Jeremy's head appeared. Never trust someone who looks around a door.

"Am I interrupting?" he asked.

"Yes," I said. I finished the call with Jimbo. Jeremy prevaricated behind the door, then entered.

"Sorry. Was it something important?" he asked, trying too hard.

"Actually, it was a gangster whose two brothers have just been murdered and I've been hired to find the perpetrator."

The truth is rarely believed. That's why it's sometimes useful. Jeremy smiled woodenly. He wanted me to ask him to sit down. I left him standing.

"I was just wondering…" he began. I looked, and decided I'd let him dig a big hole, then push himself into it. "I mean…you and I… we've often…as it were…things got off to a bad…and we never…it's a shame because…I'm sure you'd agree… all very difficult and maybe to clear the air…would you like to come out for a drink?"

"You mean on a date? You're asking me out on a date?"

"No, I don't mean…"

"What would your wife think, Jeremy?"

"My wife has nothing…I'm not…"

"I really think you should see Gwen, the counsellor. I've heard she has excellent suggestions for those in crisis. We're all a bit concerned about you, frankly. And even if I were that way inclined, I think intimate liaisons between academic staff sets a very bad example to students. Of course, I am very flattered. I'm just not interested."

All pretence dropped from Jeremy's face and he looked at me with the inviolate hatred of one possessed. This was more like it. I realized he looked like Mister Punch and half expected him to produce a hammer, and squeak "That's the way to do it, that's the way to do it!" as he battered my brains to mulch.

"You don't fool me. Everything about you is shabby and I will see you sacked. I will see you out of here and begging in the gutter for scraps of work.

I will see your life turn to ash in your mouth. If it's the last thing I do," he said, his cheeks purpling up nicely.

"Things," I said.

"What?" He asked.

"You said 'the last thing I do' but you'd already mentioned at least three things. Sacked, gutter, ash. I've got a good grammatical primer if you have problems with singular and plural."

"You grubby, pointless, little shit!" he said.

I looked at him with pained innocence. The door slammed and he was away. I hoped he didn't have a dog or cat. I knew he had a wife. I decided to drain the bottle before going to see Georgie's grave, then do battle with my former, wife-fucking friend. I wanted to take him by surprise. Before that I checked my emails and Jimbo had sent through a few photos of Georgie boy. The one I wanted, from the living room wall, showed him smiling in his 1930s suit, fedora gangster hat, all braggadocio and insouciance, and when I zoomed in I saw what I'd been hoping for. A snakeskin belt. I had another connection. Snakes.

Chapter XVI

'There are no experts in death.'
Jeff Mason

What was left of Georgie was in a small Garden of Remembrance on the other side of the crematorium to Danny. A divided family, even in death. I wanted to check the grave itself before seeing the death certificate. I was sure now that his death was connected with the recent murders of his brothers. The inscription was simple enough.

GEORGE ARNOLD STEELE (Georgie Boy)
BORN MAY 23RD 1976 DIED OCTOBER 14TH 2008
while still
He lies, as if in dewy sleep he lay;
Awake him not! surely he takes his fill
Of deep and liquid rest, forgetful of all ill.
Loved and Mourned by his Family

The whole thing was ironic. The quotation was from Shelley's *Adonais*, on the death of John Keats; it seemed that Georgie's death, far from being 'forgetful of all ill', was still casting a long and itself deadly shadow. Mick Jagger had read another part of the poem at the Stones Hyde Park Concert in 1969 after the death of Brian Jones: "Just cool it a minute. I wanna read something for Brian. .. *Peace, peace! he is not dead, he doth not sleep ...*," and in a trice Romantic poetry became rock and roll; now it had become gangster too. I wondered who chose the lines. A flash of memory, when I first met the Steeles, and Ma said that I needed to find Danny Boy's Killer as she'd promised him justice, and when I queried how you talk to the dead she had said, incongruously: "In my prayers I told him. So's he can lie peaceful, forgetful of all ill." I hadn't picked up on it but she was quoting Shelley, and from the same quotation as on Georgie's grave. Was she talking about Danny but thinking about Georgie when she said she wanted justice? And was the quotation her idea – a well hidden poetic soul in that Bavarian sow exterior? More importantly, what had happened to her fierce desire for justice? She now wanted the whole investigation ditched. Why? A lot of roads seemed to be leading back to Ma.

My knees ached and I stood suddenly to unlock my legs and shake off the earlier bottle of wine. Something, a flicker, a flit of shadow caught my eye. Someone was watching me about fifty metres away and ducked behind a gravestone. I started towards them but they knew they'd been seen and ran. They dodged in and out of graves keeping a good lead on me. Within thirty seconds my breathing was raspy, within a minute my heart strained to open like a cramped fist and I realised my commitment to taking no exercise whatsoever had paid off dividends: I was a complete physical wreck.

"Talk to me!" I shouted hoarsely but as loud as I could.

A hat flew off the figure, but I still wasn't close enough to see who it was. He was in a long coat. They reached an admin building and ran around it. I got to the building and gulped in air. They must have gone inside. I tried the door and it was open. I went inside, checking rooms: a few offices with closed doors. I opened one. An owl eyed woman looked at me curiously.

"Wrong room," I said and closed the door. To my right I could see another door out of the building. I ran to it and pushed it open in time to see a blue Mercedes leave the car park with no clear view of the driver. I traipsed back towards the grave and retrieved the hat. A new white trilby, size seven and a half, expensive, handmade in fact, by Masons of Mayfair. I would certainly be paying them a visit soon. First I had a date with another devil.

*

Wife humping bastard MP David held a surgery once a month in his constituency, Nuneaton, famous for George Eliot and giving trains a place to stop. It was meant to be a proper surgery when constituents could bring their problems and questions to him and he would earn his salary; however, David's love of his own rhetoric meant that he treated it as an opportunity to make a speech about David. Sure enough, when I opened the door to the carefully chosen utilitarian prefab, a dozen or so lost souls were seated listening to him; he appeared to think he was addressing the Nuremberg rally. He stood, the carefully arranged errant blond lock on his forehead, ready to be flicked aside for emphasis, banging on about morality: "Without a moral culture there can be no moral values...blah blah... We all have responsibilities towards ourselves, and to each other...blah blah...That's what citizenship is..." Here he sees me and falters slightly but recovers with a windy bout of finger stabbing emphasis: "That's why I vigorously support Labour's programme of zero tolerance...blah...blah...Zero tolerance of drugs, crime, and sleaze...blah blah...especially sleaze in public life. We must have leaders whom people can trust." He finished to a resounding response of indifference from his audience. People were here to talk about their failing mortgages, their inability to pay exorbitant energy bills, and to vent spleen about the crooked bankers who legally steal from our savings and wages, and not listen to some windbag.

Actually I lie, three people clapped vigorously, but I assume they were from the brain damage unit at Nuneaton General.

"Excuse me," I said.

David looked at me with barely concealed contempt sprinkled with anxiety. "Questions at the end," he said.

"Oh, I thought this was an open surgery. I didn't realise that meant zero tolerance of anyone wishing to speak."

People perked up, sensing a bit of aggro. Something real. David weighed the odds and decided on compliance. "What's your question?" he asked, smiling. Was that a line of sweat above the thin upper lip, as if a masturbating snail had recently crept along?

"It's relevant to your eloquent remarks about sleaze. Let's say it's election time and your vote counts. There are three candidates. Candidate A associates with crooked politicians and consults with astrologists. He's had two mistresses. He chain smokes and drinks eight to ten martinis every day. Candidate B was kicked out of office twice, sleeps until noon, smokes constantly, used opium in college and drinks a quart of whisky every night. Candidate C is a decorated war hero. He's a vegetarian, doesn't smoke, drinks only an occasional beer and hasn't had any extramarital affairs. Who do you vote for?"

"This is silly," said David, which was a bad move because it made him look supercilious. A few people looked at him, waiting for an answer. "I'd need to know more."

"But we have to vote without knowing the half of what you lot are up to. I bet you have secrets. Don't you?" I said, smiling.

He was trapped.

"Go on. Answer. Which one?" a man said.

"A, B or C," I added helpfully.

"I'd probably vote for C," he said.

"Congratulations," I said, "candidate A is Franklin D. Roosevelt, Candidate B is Winston Churchill, and you've just voted for Adolf Hitler as our next Prime Minister. What price zero tolerance?"

A few satisfying titters and a general air of comeuppance prevailed. David smiled benignly, which meant he wanted to kill me. My work was done here. I turned and almost fell into the arms of Lizzie. I wanted to cup her cheeks in my hands and kiss her eyelashes. She smelt of rain and vanilla and lost sunshine. I wanted to rip off her clothes and take her against the wall while she told me we were two stars who would burn brightly and crash into endless night together.

"I want you to come and clear out your stuff from the house," she said.

Such is the romantic dream. Two hours later I was just emerging from a highly charged encounter with Anna. We had promised the earth and more to each other. Undying love, everlasting desire, ludicrous devotions. She once said to me that one could say anything while having sex and it had no currency beyond that. All the words stayed in the bubble, and I knew that if she never saw me again the waters would close very quickly. It was fine. My mouth tasted of her nipples and whisky, my heart was starting to beat normally again and I felt pleasantly empty. She draped a leg languidly across my belly and smiled.

"A year of casual sex and still going strong," she said. "You could have told me you were coming round."

"I didn't know I was until I arrived."

"I might have had someone else here. What would you have done?"

"Beaten him to a pulp and thrown him over the balcony."

"Really?"

"No. Congratulated him on his excellent taste."

"Will you stay the night?"

"Yes, but not this night."

I had work to do.

Chapter XVII

'So full of artless jealousy is guilt,
It spills itself in fearing to be spilt.'
W. Shakespeare

The atmosphere at the Castle had chilled considerably. Violence and suspicion was in the air. It was the following morning and I had told Pop that someone inside the family was directly or indirectly responsible for the murders. I was interviewing the six men who lived in the castle grounds and acted as drivers, henchmen, cooks, fetchers, carriers and anything else that needed doing, legal or not. Pop watched on CCTV and then we discussed them in turn. Each felt cold until I got to the fifth, a taciturn, secretive Algerian-French guy in his early forties, Anton, pencil-thin, hook nosed, dark curly hair. He had been quite close to Georgie, but was reticent to talk of him.

"He's gone, man, what the fuck use to talk about it?"

"Tell me about him."

"He here. Now he gone."

"You were friends?"

"We hang out sometimes."

"Watch movies? DVDs?"

"Sure. Old time stuff. Black and white. Bogart, Cagney, that shit."

"You like them?"

"Sure, but Georgie crazy 'bout 'em all." He laughed abruptly. "He know their lines, man. Say them before they do. 'Top o' the world, Ma.' He love that stuff like nothing else."

"And when he died. Must have hit you hard."

Anton looked at me awry, eyes narrowed. He knew all this was going somewhere.

"Sure."

"Was there anything about his death that you thought was unusual?"

"No. What you mean?"

"He crashed into a tree at 100 mph, drunk. Those are the facts, aren't they? But what else?"

"Nothing, man," he said.

"You're lying. You don't think it was an accident. Pop wants people to tell me the truth."

He looked around, wondering if safe ground was turning to quicksand.

"He was one mean driver, Georgie. All I'm saying is, if the car hadn't been fried to cinders, it would have been worth checking the brakes. That's all. I swear I don't know nothing. It's just...he was something else with wheels."

"You think the car was fixed?"

"I don't say nothing. I do my job. The family been good to me."

I let him go and went to Pop. In his chair by the window he looked ancient in the evening sunlight as it painted his face. Like something made of translucent paper. He didn't turn to look at me. *North Utsire, South Utsire. Variable 4, becoming southerly or southeasterly 5 or 6 later. Moderate or rough. Showers. Good...*

"Interesting, but I'm really not sure it's worth spending too much time on it. We got some killer who's working his way through my family now. That's what I want stopped. Let's say Georgie's car was tampered with. Let's say that somehow it's related to the murder of two more of my sons. The trail will be warmer with Danny and Tony than Georgie so that's where you should concentrate," said Pop, almost to himself.

"OK. That's what I'll do," I said. Always agree with the paymaster, even if you have no intention of doing what you've just agreed to. As if he'd heard my thoughts, Pop wheeled his chair around to face me. "This pains me, Mister Rook," he said.

"I know."

"You may think I'm a nasty old bastard who's getting his comeuppance, but once, once…there was an evening, on a boat. Corporate thing that some ponce invited me to only because he thought I could pull strings and break bones. Bunch of tossers. There was this girl. Young. Lilac dress and legs that went on forever. Skin like….something you wanted to live in. The boat stopped down the Thames. She smiled at me, held my hand, and said 'Come on'. I mean, she did all the running. She took me onto this little island. Felt like I'd been whipped away to a magic place. Something in a kid's book. Daft. She just slipped out of her clothes like they was a silk wrap, and we went at it like beavers for half an hour. I lay there. Stars. Sweet grass. Fucking brilliant. I turned to look at her and she was gone. I goes back to the boat. Couldn't see her. Asked – where's the girl in the lilac dress? No one remembered her. Like I was the only one who saw her. Best half hour of my life. Nothing was the same after. I mean, nothing came close."

He looked at me, perhaps to see if there was a hint of mockery on my face, not caring if there was, but I was thinking of Lizzie, and a long ago time when I lay in the night with her and thought there might be something worth living for. I was fatally connected in the dark with this battered old gangster.

I told him about the film connection and he listened intently. My thinking was that the murders were by someone who was perhaps close to Georgie and was seeking revenge on his behalf and wanted me to know it, or someone was playing an elaborate game. I didn't say Ma was involved. That would start a war, with me in the middle.

"Why are you so sure Georgie's death wasn't an accident?"

I showed him the photographs of Georgie's burnt out car. He looked at the charred husk that was once his son in the driver's seat. I pointed to the roof area above the back seats. Although the car was completely burnt out you could see a dent in the roof.

"This was a new car. A Merc. Georgie loved it so I assume it would have been immaculately kept. But there's a dent here, see, at the back," I pointed.

"And...?"

"The dent goes outwards. Most dents in cars go in, where a stone or something has hit, but this was pressure from the inside."

Pop looked at me – I had his attention. "Let's say there was something in the back seat, or even under it. A small bomb, maybe home made, not enough to blow a hole but in the enclosed space the initial impact is upwards, causing this dent."

"Why wouldn't the driver get out?" he asked.

"Shock waves would have concussed him. He's groggy, probably unconscious, the car crashes, the interior is a cauldron. He dies."

"It's possible," said Pop.

There was something else, but I needed to think about it. As I left I could hear music from Philly's room – the hypnotic and deadening sounds, at least to me, of Eminem. I'd promised to tell her to be vigilant until this had stopped, one way or another. The door was ajar, so I knocked, waited, knocked, then went inside. It was a mess, more like a teenager's room. Half eaten meals on the floor, pot noodles, coke cans, clothes strewn across chairs, mugs, overflowing ash trays everywhere, unmade bed. It all spoke of a dysfunctional, confused life – a bit like mine. Something else caught my eye, a glint on the floor by the window. I picked it up. A bullet. Old fashioned. I smelt it, turned it over, then looked on the floor for more. I looked under the bed but there were just plates and mugs and a battered teddy.

I turned off the music and opened a chest of drawers and started feeling at the bottom, then I took the drawer out and looked for anything taped on the underside. In the third drawer, nestling beneath a heady assortment of pants and thongs, a gun. Luger. Pre-war. I took it out and checked the magazine. Half empty. There were other shells in the same drawer, spilling from a box of them. This weapon had been used. To kill Danny.

Chapter XVIII

'Some people never go to hell. God, what drab
lives they must lead.'
Charles Bukowski

"What the hell?!"

Jimbo was standing in the doorway. I was in his sister's bedroom, holding a loaded gun in one hand and a pair of her knickers in the other. I can see how it might look. He sat on the bed, stunned, while I told him about it. He shook his head.

"Philly. Philly! Jesus. This'll kill Pop."

"That's why we're not going to tell him." Jimbo looked sharply at me. "Yet," I added.

"Tell 'im what?" said Ma. Neither of us had heard her. Now there was no chance of keeping it quiet for a while. Ma took in everything, looked at the room in disgust and came and took the gun from my hand. She smelt the barrel. She asked where I found it and I told her under the bed. She stared at me blankly and then put the gun down and wiped a tear from her eye.

"It doesn't necessarily mean anything," I said.

Ma turned on me. "It means everything. Danny killed with a luger. How many of these do you think there are around – ones that work? I warned you. I told you. Leave it. And now look. My own daughter."

Did Ma warn me off because she suspected Philly and didn't want the awful truth to see daylight?

"What are you on about?" Jimbo asked. "What do you mean – you told him to leave it? Leave what?"

"Never you mind," said Ma.

"I'm not a kid any more, Ma," said Jimbo.

Ma turned on Jimbo and stabbed a finger in his face.

"A useless big kid is exactly what you are. Always was, always will be. This family's carried you. Without us looking out for you by now you'd be in some junkie scrapyard. 'Fink I don't know how much coke you score of a week? Useless muppet. Makes my 'eart bleed."

Jimbo was sweating heavily, the cocaine juice of a heavy user. His eyes flashed impotent hatred. "That's it. I'm out. Sod the lot of you. You won't see me again," he said.

"Good bloody riddance," said Ma.

Jimbo left, slamming the door.

"God bless," Ma said, and this time the tear was real. What the hell game was she playing?

A few moments silence.

"Your family shrinks by the hour," I said.

"Shut your gob, bloody Aristotle, and go and do something useful. Put the kettle on."

An hour later we sat in the kitchen downstairs, Ma sucking a garibaldi biscuit and dunking it in yet another mug of tea. How this charwoman came to be Queen of the foremost crime family in South England was a mystery, but she was clearly not all she seemed. I knew that now. We knew what we were waiting for – Philly's return. The luger was on the kitchen table, pointing accusingly at the door.

"Do you want to know what I think?" I said.

"No," said Ma and took another biscuit. I thought of Pop's fairy girl in a lilac dress on the river. Ten minutes later Philly appeared, looking bedraggled and tired, another night of mayhem notched up. Ma looked up at her with helpless accusation.

"Jesus, looks like another bleeding funeral," she said.

"He…" with a nod at me, "…found that in a drawer in your room," with a nod at the gun.

Philly looked at it, baffled.

"What? What would I want a gun for?"

"It's the gun that did for Danny, so you tell us why it was among your things," said Ma.

Philly looked incredulous for a moment, then gave a snort. "That is complete crap, but you know that. Ma? What's going on? Ma! I don't like it." She was starting to panic.

"Your own brother!" Ma said and got up, advancing towards Philly, who suddenly looked like a frightened little girl, backing away.

"Ma, please. You know this is a set up. I wouldn't..." and Ma cracked her on the cheek with the back of her hand; her wedding ring broke the skin in a cruel thin line, then Ma pushed past her and clomped upstairs. Philly looked at me; hurt, rage, confusion all vying for dominance in her. Then panic. "If Pop thinks I...you've got to believe me, I didn't -"

I raised a finger to my lips.

"I know you didn't. Just hang in there. I'm getting closer," I said, and left. I needed some air uncontaminated by the Steeles. As I drove away from the castle I tried to puzzle it out. There were no straight lines here. When I first found the gun there was, of course, the possibility that it belonged to Philly and she did indeed kill her own brother, maybe brothers. A moment's reflection dismissed the idea. What would she gain? Also, she was out so someone else had put on the CD in her room. Why? To make me look in and give me an opportunity to find the bullet, and then the gun. I wondered if Jimbo had planted the gun, but – no motive. They weren't close, but no one in this family was conventionally close. It was possible that whoever had gone into her room before when she was in the shower had returned, but I knew that wasn't the case. I knew exactly who had planted the gun – Ma. She was in the house, and so could have put on the CD to gain my attention. She'd also suggested earlier that I speak to Philly. Most tellingly, when she asked where I found the gun I lied and said under the bed, yet when she confronted Philly she said I'd found it in her drawer; Ma knew exactly where the gun was because she put it there. Why would she frame her own daughter? They hated each other but was that enough to make her look like a murderer? And to do that so hot on the heels of asking me to quit the case. Perhaps she framed Philly in the hope that I'd believe it and would quit. Was it that Ma was frightened of more murders, as she'd said, or was she trying to deflect attention from me finding the real murderer? Did Ma know who it was? In any case, I needed to visit a hat shop.

Chapter XIX

'There was of course no way of knowing whether you were being watched at any given moment.'
George Orwell

He looked touchingly like someone from another age: Edwardian, the high noon of Englishness before the industrialized slaughter of World War 1. Freud had cracked open the unconscious and Nietzsche was sitting in a nursing home looking at the white space inside his skull; innocence, if it ever existed, was a fading dream, but England was enjoying a 1911 summer. This hat man had a blue and white spotted bow tie, a bold checked waistcoat and a music hall smile that followed the wing span of his peppery moustache to bold dimensions. A smell of violet cachous hovered around him. I imagined his name was Eustace, or Brimley.

"I found this hat," I said.

His eyebrows shot up and nearly left his head. He looked at the hat as if it was a naked nun. "I see," he said, drawing out the *ee* for emphasis.

"You see what?" I asked.

"I see that, having found this hat, you have exerted yourself in preliminary enquiries, ascertaining not only the maker, i.e. me, but the precise geographical whereabouts of the maker. Not content with this you have taken the time, trouble and expense to pursue those enquiries to their logical conclusion, my shop. I see from that, barring fetishistic obsessions with hat singular or hats plural, you must have a specific reason for being here. As such, this hat is a synecdoche, I use the term loosely and not with grammatical precision – but it represents something more than itself. Therefore I see that you will ask more questions, which could range from 'I love this hat and will you make me one?' – unlikely as you are more of a cranially naked man, a head unflattered by millinery endeavour, and therefore to the more likely 'Who does it belong to?' variety. Am I getting warm?"

I loved this man.

"Who does it belong to?" I asked.

"I couldn't possibly tell you. We are akin to the legal and medical professions. Client confidentiality."

I took out a hundred pounds in twenties and put them on the counter. He never looked at the notes, merely covered them with the hat and they disappeared.

"Tuesday afternoon is accounts. I therefore produce my accounts ledger," and with that he brought out a dusty ledger from beneath the counter that even Bob Cratchit would have scoffed at. "Remembering a sudden miniature crisis in my little kitchen, let's venture a crumpet unbuttered, a scone uncreamed and jammed, I leave for a moment, leaving a curious someone, if there be such a one, to peruse said accounts ledger, probably under the letter O. And with that he left the room." Which he did. I turned to O and after a few flick throughs there it was. Charles O'Bannion who bought a white trilby two months ago. O'Bannion. The name scratched around in my mind. I googled it on my iPhone. James Cagney based his performance of Tom Powers in *Public Enemy* on real Chicago gangster Charles Dion O'Bannion and two New York City hoodlums he had known as a youth. The address was 2B Spenser Rd in Norwood.

Reluctantly I left my new best friend and stepped outside into the wicked world. An hour later I rang the doorbell of the mysterious Charles Dion O'Bannion. No answer. I rang again and an upstairs window opened. A man with no chin to speak of – his head just dissolved into his neck, and a combover of thin black strands looked out.

"I'm looking for Charles. Mr O'Bannion," I said.

"He's not here."

"No, I gather that. Any idea when he'll be back?"

"Only comes round a couple of times a week. Who wants to know?"

"I'm an insurance agent."

"You don't look insurance," he said suspiciously.

"What does insurance look like?" I asked.

"Not like you."

"It's motor insurance. Someone's making a claim against him. His blue Merc."

"Nice car that. How much is the insurance on it?"

"Too much, he'd say. I just need to check I've got the right person. If I show you a photograph…"

"No point. He always comes at night. Wears a hat. Never actually seen him up close."

"Can I interest you in any insurance? We've got some good deals on private health at the moment."

The window closed instantly. I still didn't know where my guardian angel lived, but at least I knew a place he visited. I went home to shower and change. Cass was eating chocolate ice cream and watching Jeremy Kyle, a sure sign of clinical depression. I kissed her on the head.

"What is it?" I asked.

"Everything," she said.

"That's nice and specific."

"Mum's livid with you for making David look a prat."

"I didn't have to try hard."

"Tregown keeps sending you emails. Wants to see you urgently."

"I'll pop in some time. How often do you look at my emails."

"Twice a day."

"Even the personal ones?"

"Especially the personal ones. There was one from the woman you're knocking off that was filthy so I deleted it. Don't want your computer, or anything else, infected. I need a decent quotation for my essay. Something that suggests everything is relative. All stuff about right and wrong, good and bad. It's all made up."

"For there is nothing either good or bad, but thinking makes it so…*Hamlet*, Act two, scene two. And throw in a few quotations from Nietzsche's *Beyond Good and Evil*. Your final paragraph should have something about the Law being based on a construct, a palace of beliefs, opinions and concepts that have no absolute intrinsic value, but without which society would fall apart."

"And that's a bad thing?"

"As you say, it's all relative, Cass. Some days I pray to the god of Chaos for society to implode. More importantly, I need you to do something for me. When a body is burnt to death, does the skeletal structure change shape significantly?"

She smiled at me as if I'd just given her an exquisite flower. She's strange like that, which is one of many reasons I adore her. She busied herself while I checked local records and found that 2B Spenser Rd was owned by a company called Omega Housing. I rang them but it was a recorded message. I checked out Omega Housing in Company Records and found it was an offshoot company of another housing company called Nelson Developments. On the Board of Directors was one N. Steele. Ma's name was Nora. Circles within circles. I went back to watch the flat rented by the mysterious Charles O'Bannion. I parked across the road and sat re-reading Sartre's *Being and Nothingness* for a lecture I would probably cancel entitled *Suicide as a Way of Defeating Mortality*. Three hours later I was awoken in the dark by the message beep on my iPhone: **Missed me again**. I looked around but the road was empty. I looked up at the flat but there were no lights on. I was in a chess game where I kept getting checked.

Chapter XX

'Of all the things that wisdom provides to help one live one's entire life in happiness, the greatest by far is the possession of friendship.'
Epicurus

"It's partly a question of temperature. The skeletal structure remains more or less intact unless it gets absolutely nuked," said Cass.

"That's what I thought. In which case, look at this," I said, and brought up the picture of Georgie's burnt out car.

Cass scrutinized it.

"What am I looking for?"

"Inconsistencies. Look at the body." I enlarged the image of the body.

"Fried," Cass said.

"What do people in cars do?"

"Drive."

"And how do they do that?"

"Steer, look at the road, work the pedals...Hang on, how could they...?"

"Exactly," I said, "the feet don't go anywhere near the pedals. Even allowing for shoes burning off..."

"Maybe the seat got pushed back in the blast?" Said Cass.

"Maybe. Or he wasn't driving. Think about it. The Steeles keep everything under wraps. The accident wasn't properly investigated. I bet the body, such as it is, wasn't identified properly. He's wearing Georgie's ring, but that doesn't mean anything."

"You think Georgie's still alive? But why would he set this up?"

"I can think of several reasons, but first we have to find out if he really is alive. What?" Cass was giving me a curious look.

"You said 'We'."

"Slip of the tongue."

"You don't make slips of the tongue."

"You've been a great help, Cass. Thank you."

"I could help you find Georgie."

"Please, leave that to me."

She chewed her lip and flicked a stray lock of hair back.

"On one condition," she said eventually.

I waited.

"You at least go into Uni today. Just to show your face. I'm worried you'll lose your job," she said.

"I'm touched at your concern," I said.

"Don't be. If you're out of a job who pays my fees?"

"OK. Deal," I said. I could have said that in a profession like academia that includes more than a usual quota of lazy, complacent, self deluding, humourless, bitter morons, the chances of me being sacked were a thousand to one. And if I went down I'd take a hell of a lot with me. My hacking hobby meant that I had access to the dirty linen of half the campus: porn, chat lines, absenteeism, secret liaisons, affairs with students, debts, rivalries, threats – there was no shoddy little vice that didn't exist in that architecturally offensive, windswept little factory.

To honour my deal with Cass I went to the university. I printed off a few fliers saying my seminars were cancelled for the next week. My door opened and Jeremy came in. I could tell by the patronizing smile that he'd had what he foolishly thought was a good idea.

"I've had several complaints about you, Doctor Rook," he said. I carried on printing my fliers. "Serious complaints," he added darkly. I started to make a coffee. "I thought you'd want to know the nature of the complaints," he said. I opened my filing cabinet, wondering what the hell was in there. A bottle of whisky nestled enticingly in the Research file. Jeremy's attempt to corral and intrigue, even scare me, was predictably failing and I could see in the corner of my eye that he was starting to boil nicely. My main complaint about the man was that he was no serious challenge.

"Could you stop fiddling about and listen!" he shouted.

I sat down and looked at him.

"The complaints are about you ridiculing the personal and deeply held religious beliefs of some students. I know that, despite being an atheist, you would want to answer these complaints by offering a platform for fair and rational debate about faith systems, and given the faculty's commitment to interdisciplinary teaching and horizontal pedagogies, I am putting you down to teach the Philosophy of Religion core course for the rest of term, starting next week." He paused, triumphant.

I gave him my most indifferent stare.

"Have you any questions?"

"No. That's fine, Jeremy, and thank you for this opportunity to teach something close to my heart. It's a bit of a dream come true." I went back to my filing cabinet and started whistling *Fur Elise*. He hovered uncertainly for a good thirty seconds, then slammed the door.

*

I rang Jimbo's mobile number. He sounded stoned. His walk through the fire was a very shaky one at the best of times and I thought that probably he'd have a complete collapse within the next year. I asked him about his childhood with his siblings – what they did, where they went. At first annoyed, he settled, with the aid of a joint or a crack pipe, to judge from the occasional deep inhalations and increasing soporific tone to his voice, into a rambling reminiscent monologue. It all sounded hideous, mostly rivalries, fights, squabbles, jockeying for parental affection and attention. There was one bright spot – a place called Chatworth Manor, long ago abandoned by minor aristocrats who couldn't pay their debts and, like all royals, wouldn't consider working for a living. Jimbo suddenly became animated and said it was one of the few times when he, Georgie, Danny and Philly would be free of Tony and would play hide and seek, war, cowboys and Indians and, Georgie's favourite – gangsters. One golden summer of halcyon days. It was worth a visit.

Chapter XXI

'...the living spring from the dead, and that the
souls of the
dead are in existence.'
Socrates

I parked in a lane on the perimeter. The fences and huge wrought iron scrolled gates were rusty but intact. A weather beaten sign said UNDER DEVELOPMENT, but there were no signs of it. I slipped through the fence, across an overgrown paddock and into a thick wood, years of fallen leaves and pulped timber mulched to a soft carpet. This would be a paradise for kids, an enchanted place such as probably covered most of England a thousand years ago: a time of bears and boars, briars, oaks and elms, beech wood, fungi like triffids, a lot of wild berries, smells of peat and damp leaves where sunlight never played. To have been alive before things were given names must have been extraordinary – everything a mystery, the world full of dangers and possibilities. Perhaps humans were not so ludicrously self entranced then.

Suddenly the wood finished and there, across what may have once been a croquet lawn but was now a confusion of nettles, mole hills, wild flowers and, incongruously, at least a dozen abandoned prams and a rusting metal bed frame, was a ruined mid-nineteenth century manor house, solid and square but with two castellated towers, one of which was peppered with rook nests and looked about to tumble given a breath of wind.

I approached it, pushed open the door to the great hall where I was greeted by hundreds of minute flutterings as disturbed bats resettled. Stumps of great Dorian columns that once supported a frescoed ceiling, decaying rafters and collapsed upper floors made up the decor. I imagine the original was a colourful mix of gothic and neo-classical at a moment of high romanticism. The dead who once lived here perhaps thought that even if they didn't live for ever, their possessions would. I heard a skittering behind, but could see nothing in the gloom. I walked across the hall, the debris of a hundred vagrant parties littering the floor – cheap wine bottles, cans, pizza cartons. Ironic that the dregs of society partied in what was once the sole enclave of the privileged few.

I looked up from the foot of a decrepit staircase and tested it with my foot. It crumbled to dust. The whole place was rotten with woodworm. More skittering and behind me a large rat stood on its haunches, its glittering eyes unafraid. There was a kitchen down a few concrete steps with things growing in what were once sinks, thick curtains of spider webs, the smell of death and things rotting. Inside an ancient cupboard a rat was eating something – a dead bird or another rat. I pulled the rope of a dumb waiter and the whole carapace crashed down – instantly the room was a thick dust cloud. I was suddenly spooked and had to get out. It felt as if something malevolent was waiting there, staring from shadowed corners. I turned and ran straight into a huge clinging web that closed around me like cling film. I panicked and clawed it away and ran through the great hall, stumbling over fallen bricks. I had to get out.

Outside I took great lungfuls of air and felt foolish. At least I'd determined that no one was staying in the house. It was a long shot thinking Georgie would be there. Perhaps he really was dead. I went back through the woods, feeling the instant chill. I passed a large oak and something clicked. A broken twig? No, I knew that sound. I stopped, knowing there was a gun a few inches behind my head. I turned, enough to see a gloved hand and brown suited arm holding a luger pistol.

"Don't turn around." The voice was London working class, but with a hint of Brooklyn. "We're not gonna be strangers. Walk."

I started walking slowly ahead.

"What you want to run out on me for? We're together, aren't we?"

"If you say so," I said.

Whoever it was suddenly got very angry. "No! No! You just say 'Sure.' Sure. Say it."

"Sure," I said.

We had taken a hidden path and were walking deeper into the woods. I assumed there wasn't a picnic of cucumber sandwiches and chilled Chablis waiting at the end. It struck me, not for the first time, how ludicrous it was for human beings to be so compliant when they feel they are about to be clipped. Hitler knew that and murdered practically a whole people. Terror subdues us. The man behind me started half singing, half humming, to himself: "I'm forever blowing...dee dee dee dee dee dee dee...they fly so high...dee dee dee dee dee...then like your dreams they fade and die..."

I wanted to quote from Hamlet or Macbeth to take my mind away, but I thought this would annoy him even more. He kept up his private monologue. In a little clearing we arrived at a dilapidated cottage. The gun prodded me in the back and I opened the door. We were in a small lounge with gangster film posters on all the walls – Cagney, Bogart, Raft – a

TV, shelves of DVDs (probably all gangster films, I surmised) and a couple of moth eaten armchairs. It was a fan's room. This was definitely Georgie, or a clone of his.

"OK. Turn and no sudden moves."

I turned. He had his head down, and was wearing a white homburg hat similar to the one Cagney wore in *White Heat*, a brown pin striped old fashioned wide lapelled suit, collar up, and shiny black and white shoes. Slowly he looked up and even with the wide brim shadowing his face I could see he was horribly scarred from serious burns, one eye displaced, the skin raw looking, molten.

"Now tell me you're glad to see me, tell me low, so nobody can hear," he said. Most of what he said, perhaps all, were lines from gangster films. This man was completely away with the fairies, except the fairies wore baggy suits and killed people.

"I'm pleased to see you," he said. He smiled lopsidedly, then raised the gun to my head. "I'm going to have to give it to you. Smack between the eyes."

Chapter XXII

'Freedom of choice is an illusion. You have no choice. You have owners.'

George Carlin

Georgie looked at me curiously, then tensed his finger on the trigger, ready to squeeze. Close up I could see that his face had almost melted in the fire. Much of the skin was smooth and raw looking.

"Is this a dagger which I see before me,

The handle toward my hand? Come, let me clutch thee: -

I have thee not, and yet I see thee still…"

He hesitated and looked perplexed. I carried on.

"I have supp'd full with horrors; direness, familiar to my slaught'rous thoughts, cannot once start me…Have you seen it?"

"Seen what?"

"*Joe Macbeth*. A gangster take on Macbeth. Set at the racetrack. Directed by Ken Hughes."

Georgie's good eye lit up. "1955. Paul Douglas as Joe Macbeth," he said.

"Ruth Roman as Lily Macbeth," I said.

"Bonar Colleano as Lennie."

"Sid James as Banky."

"Harry Green as Big Dutch," said Georgie, and lowered the gun. He was lost in the film, as if it was playing out before his eyes.

"I like your hat. Do you remember the cap Cagney wears in *Public Enemy*?" I said.

Georgie touched his hat. Then he ran to a dresser, opened a drawer and took out a replica cap. He still had his gloves on, presumably to hide burns. He put on the cap and took off the white hat – his head was ribbed and puckered and pinky bald from burns, except one long strand of hair that flopped over the crown. "'I wish you was a wishin' well, so's I could tie a bucket around you and sink you,' snarls gangster Tom Powers, to his complaining moll, Kitty. Then, assuring himself a place in cinema history, the surly Cagney picks up a grapefruit and shoves it right in her face. Splat. That's one of my favourite scenes."

"Cagney. The cockiness," I said, realising that if I could keep Georgie talking he might not kill me.

"The sandpaper charm," said Georgie.

"Lightning reflexes."

"High calibre sneer."

"Ultimate tough guy."

"There's not much for supper. All the peanut butter's gone. I probably won't shoot you tonight. Give me your phone," he said, his tone suddenly switching. I gave him my iPhone. Cass would start to worry if I didn't answer my phone some time this evening. I just hoped she wouldn't go out looking for me.

I wondered what would happen when the novelty wore off for Georgie of having someone to discuss gangster films with. He was oddly childlike, yet this was a cold blooded killer who seemed to be working his way through the gruesome murder of his siblings. He had to be intelligent to plan the way he had, and to keep tabs on me without tripping up. I thought that as long as we stayed in his fantasy gangster world I might be safe. I ached with questions about his faked death, about his life since and why he was on this mission of death, but clearly to ask anything yet would be akin to suicide.

Suddenly he switched and pointed the gun at me. He took three DVDs from a shelf.

"You get to choose which DVD we watch," he said. "Choose right and we have a tickety boo movie night. Choose wrong and you get a gift from Mister Luger here, smackeroo between the eyes," pointing the gun at my head and making little shooting gestures. "Pow, pow, pow."

"You like lugers?" I asked

"Got a batch on 'em in a drawer. Not bulky, y'see."

He held up each DVD in turn. *The Maltese Falcon. Public Enemy. The Big Heat.* I did a mock eeny meeny miny mo, and felt the adrenalin pulse. When everything hangs in the balance something happens to time. It becomes perfumed, almost palpable, as you realise you may soon be denied it for good. I knew which film to choose, but bizarrely, stupidly, I wanted to savour the moment, the possibility of being wrong. What mattered in the moment? Darling Cass. My bitch wife whom I loved and hated. Seeing my father, just once. My mum in a nursing home and whom I never visit now. Why? Laziness and selfishness? Probably, but also to avoid the pain of watching her disappear memory by memory, word by word, recognizable objects becoming mysteries, others a constant gallery of strangers; Nietzsche – the moment when his mind slipped away, a kind of death in itself. I was in love with Sisyphus. I was also being a complete idiot.

"Come on, little Rooky. Choose," he said.

"Has to be, no two ways, *Public Enemy*," I said.

He made as if to shoot me, then grinned, the bad eye disappearing in folds of puckered, burnt flesh. "I'll get the popcorn," he said.

We settled in the armchairs and ate from two huge buckets of popcorn while we watched *Public*

Enemy. Georgie knew every line of dialogue, every gesture, and either mimed them or said the lines with the characters. It was very annoying. We got to the bar scene, with Putty Nose singing as Cagney and his buddy walk through. Georgie started singing, "Lizzie Jones, big and fat, slipped on the ice and broke her...." then he whistled and giggled. His mood swings were pronounced, as if a new track was switched on and he became different versions of himself.

When the film finished he looked at me a long time, as if weighing up all kinds of possibilities. He locked the door to the cottage.

"Tomorrow I finish you. It has to be. It's written," he said.

"Where is it written?" I asked.

He tapped his head. "Lots of good stuff here," he said. "Scripts, stories, characters. But you got tonight to think how you wanna go. Any death from any film. You choose and it's yours tomorrow at sunrise. *Godfather* movies have lots of possibilities. Garroting. Bullet through the eye. Or there's the weird stuff. Snake down the gullet in *Collateral*. You choose. Me – I'd go for something traditional. But it's your goodbye, Rooky. I sleep light, so don't try to fly." He went to what I could see was a tiny adjoining room that had a mattress on the floor. He even closed the door, so sure was he of this little scene he'd created. There was a tiny bathroom off this main room too. I went and splashed my face with water.

Bizarrely I found myself actually considering which film death I'd choose. Perhaps Georgie was really very clever and knew that, having planted the thought, it would keep circling in my mind. I'd also had enough experience of him to know that he didn't work in a straightforward manner. There would be some twist to everything he said and did.

It was going to be a long night.

Chapter XXIII

'Anger…there is no swifter way to insanity.'
Seneca

It was midnight. Cass would have gone through the motions of wondering whether or not to call the police, whether to let her mother know. I don't go in for close friends so her options were limited. She might contact Anna who would be mystified. I hoped she wouldn't go to the Steeles. That could only make things difficult for her. All adrenalin had gone and I was no longer excited about being imprisoned in the middle of nowhere by a psychopathic killer with a film fetish. But even now, one of my overriding feelings was of curiosity. I wanted to know Georgie's story from the inside. Something about being able to squeeze others' lives into a coherent narrative, because my own is always shadowy, partial fragments jostling in the night. My mother's silver painted hairbrush on a glass shelf. An old dog called Rossie with her seventh or eighth litter of pups tumbling behind her. A photograph of my father, in profile and looking intently at a pier in the distance; what was this? A day at the seaside. A rare treat when he and my mother were together? With Photoshop I've tried to turn the photograph around and recompose his face, but it doesn't work. I can't see the man, only my own projections and the limits of technology.

At 2 am my wheels were starting to come off. I needed a drink. I needed to get away. The windows were locked but they were old and rusty framed. I tried one and could see that it would give fairly easily. I pulled slightly and it started to come away from the wall. I stopped and listened. Nothing. I eased the window a little more. Some plaster fell away and the hinge was exposed. Then a click behind me.

"I was just trying to get some air," I said.

"Sit down and shut up, you dirty double-crossing rat," said Georgie, borrowing the famous Cagney phrase. I turned and sat. He stood looking at me. "I'm disappointed," he said, "I give you a whole night to decide how you want to die. Do you realise what a privilege that is? Mister Death usually just steals up from nowhere and pow, you're gone. No time to think. You had a chance to be different, and you blew it. I am so bloody angry!"

I was deafened and fell backwards as he fired a shot into the wall. Until you have been really close to a gunshot you have no idea what a powerful, penetrating and painful sound it is. I have never got used to it. The sheer brutal finality of the blast. He sat looking at me. In his hat and gloves it was difficult not to think I was in some strange denouement scene in a twilight drama and would awaken from it. My ears were still smarting from the gunshot. He took a Mars bar from his pocket and started eating it.

"From now on, the rules are off! I'm gonna talk when I please and do what I like. I'm gonna be as mean and dirty and hard to handle as the worst con in the joint and I'll skull-drag any rat or screw that gets in my way, do you hear?" he said, suddenly animated.

"From *Each Dawn I Die*. Cagney plays a wrongly convicted reporter. Is that what galls you, Georgie, the injustice of everything?" I asked.

He looked at me, his good eye searching for an answer to something.

"What led you to me?" he asked.

"The film deaths, the Merc, the snake references, and the guy in the burnt car wasn't you," I said.

"Clever sod."

"You too. Why did you keep saving my neck?" I asked.

He smiled. "You'll work it out. I played you. But I don't always know. I get news but...I don't always believe it. What's Pop like now?" he asked.

"Ill. Haunted. Had a mild heart attack or stroke over the death of Danny. He's ripe for another now that Tony's gone and Jimbo left."

He looked. "Jimbo gone? I wasn't told. Where?"

"I don't know. Told by whom?" I asked.

He ignored the question. He was thinking about Jimbo. "Probably Spider's gaff. If that's where he gets his gear still. If he's off 'is face he'll go somewhere familiar. Now Tony's gone..." he trailed off into thought.

I asked him why he didn't kill Philly too when he had the chance.

"We was close, me and her. I couldn't do it. Besides, it wasn't her I was after. You think I'm nuts? You think I'm a crazeee...?"

"No, I think you're behaving perfectly rationally. You want revenge. Tony wanted you out of the way because Pop said he wouldn't necessarily take over the family. Suddenly brothers are enemies. And you were next in line. All you're doing is what Kings and Queens and politicians have been doing since civilization began. Someone gets in the way – you get rid of them. You're not nuts. The world is. What really happened, Georgie?"

This was it. The moment. He exhaled heavily, as if he'd been punctured.

"In the car. Me and my mate Lenny Barnes. No one knew he was with me, little Lenny. Tony left a package on the back seat. Asked us to take it to the post. It blew. Felt me skin was melting. Lenny copped it worst. Died straight away. I pushed him in the driver's seat and got out. Rolled down into a stream. Even then, with all the pain, I was planning – let him think I'm dead. Let him think it's me. Came here. Then I started to think they was all in it. Danny Boy, Tony, Jimbo, even Pop. Get me out of the way. So, I thought I'd do 'em, one by one, ending with Pop. Scupper the Steeles. The whole male line."

"Makes sense, but what then?"

"Then it's over. You know, there's hardly ever any difference between things."

"I don't understand," I said.

"Us. The Steeles. We could've been fucking gippos or grocers or on the social, instead of kings of shit hill. We were kings but it all came at a price. To me, it meant being somebody in a neighbourhood full of nobodies, but it could have easily cut either way. You know, Cagney was going to play the good guy in Public Enemy. The line is cut feather thin between good and fucked up. Have you decided how you want to die yet?"

"Yes. I want to die of a peaceful heart attack at night when I'm eighty eight years old and asleep," I said.

He laughed.

"I like you, Rooky, but one way or another you're popped."

He aimed the gun at me. Now it was certain I felt curiously detached. All the unfinished things dissolved as I realised every life has things undone, half achieved, partially resolved. What the hell, really? It doesn't matter. I wished I could see Cass one last time. I wished I could make Lizzie utterly miserable one last time. I had a sudden flash and was back at school, in the unpainted, pee and bleach smelling toilets, other boys mocking me:

1ST BOY: You ain't got a Dad, Rook.

ME: Yes I do.

1ST BOY: Who is he, then?

ME: Jack the Ripper, Springheel Jack, the man with the snakes who shakes you awake...

BOYS: (Laugh)

I thought once the laughter stopped I'd hear another shot, and I'd stop. Then the door opened and Ma walked in with a bag of Tesco groceries.

Chapter XXIV

'They fuck you up, your mum and dad.
They may not mean to, but they do.
They fill you with the faults they had
And add some extra, just for you..'
Philip Larkin

She took in the scene very quickly and planted the groceries on a small rickety table.

"Best put down the shooter and make a cuppa. Bloody jingly-jungly out there and I'm parched," she said.

Georgie wavered though clearly he was still his mother's boy, and he put down the gun, while making a mock shoot at me with a finger and thumb behind her back. Ma sat down, opened a packet of garibaldi and put her feet up on a chair. She eyed me as a weasel would a duckling.

"Couldn't keep your nose out of it," she said, and sniffed contemptuously. Beneath the bravado was an elderly, exhausted woman. I'd been doing a lot of rapid thinking. Already I knew that Georgie was Ma's favourite so presumably she conspired to keep his survival a secret in case Tony tried to kill him again. Then when Georgie started murdering his brothers she had a real problem – if she couldn't stop him she had to protect him, but how far and at what cost? She didn't want him found – that's why she said at the flat that she wanted me to stop, and not because she thought the murders would stop. But there was one unthinkable part of the puzzle. She set up Philly by planting the gun.

"Why put the gun in Philly's room?" I asked, unable to help myself.

"You probably think what kind of old bitch would make her daughter look like she murdered her own brother. Answer is – this old bitch. I knew it wouldn't stick, but it would buy time until…I could find a way out," she said.

I realised something else. "You were horrible to Jimbo so that he'd leave. Get him out of the way of…" I indicated Georgie. Ma smiled. Always a reason for her nastiness.

"What a family," I said.

"At least we are a family. What's left? What have you got, Mister clever bollocks?"

"Nothing much," I said.

"Nothing much is what you are then," she said.

"I have to tell Pop about all this," I said. "He's not going to be happy with you."

She snorted. "When was he ever? But you can't tell 'im nothing."

Georgie passed her a mug of tea, me another. He picked up the gun again.

"So let me pop him, Ma. Solves the problem."

"No. It don't. 'Is kid knows 'e's connected to us, which probably means a dozen others do. 'E goes tits up the bill is round before we know it. I've thought about it." She eyed me. I was starting to feel sorry for Pop, married to this biscuit eating walrus with a heart of lead. "Pop paid you to find the killer. And you feel bound to finish the job, right?"

I nodded. It was something like that.

"You did what you was paid to do. You found 'im. Nothing was said about having to talk about it. You done your job. Now I'm paying you..." she took a fat parcel from a carrier bag, "...fifty grand to fuck off. That's your new job. Capiche?"

It was a lot of money. I could set up a Trust fund for Cass. I could buy a gold plated bear trap and put David's head in it. I was a man with scruples, but with fifty grand I could buy some new ones. I reached out and took the package.

"You're going to keep Georgie here a secret still?" I asked.

"He's going abroad. New start. Argentina or somewhere. Pop'll never know. Now you've been paid. Sling it."

I left the cottage and could hear Georgie remonstrating with Ma. He came running after me. Ma stood helplessly at the door watching.

"Georgie! Son!" she shouted.

I stopped. He didn't have the gun. He stopped before me, looking like a helpless plastic baby. He'd never cope with anything like a normal life. Ma might be clever, but she was delusional about Georgie, blinded by warped love.

"It's all gone wrong," he said. "Why'd you think I let you find me?"

I had no idea. Because you're crazy? I thought. He was getting agitated. I suddenly realised.

"You needed an ending, didn't you? For the film you're in." I said.

He beamed. "Yeh yeh yeh! All good gangster films the gangster gets caught or shot in the end. Even if I shot you somehow the police would arrive and pow pow the shoot out. The big payoff. 'Cos of the good guy. That's you."

"If you think I'm the good guy you're really screwed, Georgie," I said, and turned away. In a peculiar way it felt like abandoning him. He didn't have an ending. Ma was right. In this line of work when I've been paid I like to see it through, so I went straight to the bank, deposited the money in a safe box and pocketed the key. Then I went home. Cass was sitting on the sofa twisting her hair the way she does when she's in crisis. She looked at me accusingly, then fell in my arms. Her hair smelled like life.

"I'm so scared I'm going to lose you one day," she said.

"Not today, Cassie. Today I buy you lunch. Somewhere classy."

"My choice then?" she asked, looking at me.

"Absolutely."

"Macdonald's," she said. Hoisted on my own petard. An hour later, having feasted on bad coffee and fat, I took Cass to Lizzie's and dropped her outside. I said I had to visit my mother in hospital. It's true that I had to – any half decent son would acknowledge that, but I hadn't told Cass that was what I was actually going to do. Because I wasn't. It wasn't strictly a lie and, in any case, there was a truth involved. The truth I was on my way to tell Pop Steele.

Chapter XXV

'...for this my son was dead, and is alive again; he was lost,
and is found. And they began to be merry.'
The Parable of the Prodigal Son
Luke 15:24 King James Bible

Ma was in the kitchen and only realised I was in the house when she turned and saw me at the foot of the stairs. Her eyes startled but she wasn't quick enough; I was in Pop's room before she could catch me. The curtains were drawn against the sun. He looked smaller, dysthimically shrunken, but the eyes still glittered in the shadows as he lightly drummed his fingers to the incantatory lullaby of "Fisher, German Bight Cyclonic, five to seven. Moderate or rough. Rain or showers. Good, occasionally poor..." He indicated a chair and I sat and waited. He turned down the sound.

"I sense more bad news," he said.

"I know who murdered your sons," I said.

"Georgie. My boy."

I wasn't expecting this.

"You knew?"

"Came to suspect. I check everything, even grocery bills; it's why I'm so successful. I found one in Ma's purse that had three jars of crunchy peanut butter and a dozen Mars bars. Georgie's favourites."

"So why hire me?"

"When I hired you I didn't know. Not a bleedin' clue. Now I do. I knew you were good. I knew you'd be right. Tell me."

"He was horribly injured. It was Tony. He planted a bomb in the car. That's why Georgie's on this mission of revenge."

Pop ran a liver-spotted, gnarled hand over his thin, exhausted hair. "Why did he wait so long?" he asked.

"It took him a long time to heal, and he probably did nothing but watch DVDs – they connected in his mind with his desire for payback. It's all snarled up together. I don't think he always knows what's real and what's from a film."

"While his bloody mother fed him and allowed it all to fester." He raised his voice. "You can come in now."

The door opened and Ma entered. She looked knives at me, then at Pop. "If you knew, why didn't you help me, you bloody old goat?" she asked, her eyes filling, wanting to strike him. He smiled, perhaps at the power he still had to frustrate and annoy her. Perhaps it was increasingly all he had left. Then he shook his head wearily. "That's why. We can't get nothing right between us."

Ma looked at me. "Bloody Judas! You took my money. You said if you take the money you do the job. Liar."

I took out the key for the bank deposit box and put it on the table. "The key to a deposit box. The whole fifty grand is there. In the name of Jimmy Cagney. You can collect it when you like."

She put pride in her pocket and took the key. "So what now?" she asked.

"You know what now, Ma. Call him. Call the prodigal home. Now. This has to finish before we do," and Pop handed the phone to Ma.

She hesitated then dialled a number. "It's me. Pop knows. Come to the Castle. Yes, of course now. It's all right."

Then we waited. Pop listened to the shipping forecast. I sipped a large scotch. Ma fretted and kept looking through the window that faced the long drive below. I left and went to Philly's room and knocked. Loud music blared from inside – Sid Vicious singing *My Way*, just before shooting his mother in the film *The Great Rock and Roll Swindle*. This was Philly's Mantovani. I opened the door and she lay on the bed, looking at the ceiling and chain smoking. I turned down the music and told her about Georgie. She appeared not to be listening, then she turned to me and giggled, which bubbled into a full laugh. A helpless laugh that rocked her. The laugh became an eye watering cough. Inappropriate behaviour. Cognitive dissonance. Fear of one's own emotions. Not knowing how to respond to things. Schizoid. Yes, laughter made absolute sense in the crippled geography of Philly's mind.

"Oh Jesus, even the dead ones in our family come back to slaughter the rest," she said. "We're like the fucking Addams Family."

I left her to what passed in her mind for thinking and went back to join Pop. I wondered how far we really were from Endgame. I was on my third scotch when Pop suddenly banged his fist down on a table, turned to Ma and shouted "I told him to come now! Ring him again." I could see how, in younger days, he would have been a forbidding figure, and how the kids would try not to rile him. Like all kings his reign was almost over, with perhaps a few twists left. Lear in the last Act. Ma telephoned.

"Answerphone," she said, then left a message, "Son, please come home. Where are you?"

Moments later her phone peeped with a text alert. She looked at me, then Pop.

"What's he say?"

"Says: Ask Rooky. 'e knows where."

They both looked at me accusingly.

"If you're playing a game here, if you're playing a game, you're delivered home tonight in bits. They'll call you Rook tikka, after my people have sliced, diced and charcoaled you," said Pop.

I turned to Ma. "You were there. You saw. He wanted to shoot me. How the hell do I know where he is?"

"Then why the monkey's arse is 'e saying you do?" Ma said.

A good question and I needed an answer quickly. I thought I might have one. "OK, I think I know what he means, but I might be wrong, and you won't like it anyway," I said.

"Mister Rook, I don't like anything much at this moment, so you got nothing to lose," said Pop.

I hoped I wasn't putting a noose around my own neck. I also enjoyed the fear of the moment, the whisky settling in, the sweat on my neck. I thought I might suddenly throw up, but swallowed the sensation. The carpet was expensive and I could never afford the cleaning bill.

"OK. All this family stuff is bound up with gangster films in Georgie's mind. I think the crash and his horrific injuries have jumbled to the extent that he can only makes sense of what he does in terms of a film, a story. This one is a classic. Rags to riches. Crime family drama. Sibling rivalry. Thwarted ambition. Betrayals. Dominating parents – no insult intended. Revenge. It's Jacobean. It has all the huge themes. It gives Georgie a ready-to-wear identity, a role, and a sense of coherence that real life can never have."

"Is this psycho-twat crap leading anywhere? What does it mean?" Ma asked. Pop silenced her with a contemptuous look.

"What it means is that the story dominates everything Georgie does. And he told me what the story is for him. As he was healing from the crash he started to think all the men in his family were in a conspiracy against him. He said: 'So, I thought I'd do 'em, one by one, ending with Pop. Scupper the Steeles. The whole male line.'"

"You mean he won't stop 'til he's done us all. Jimbo. Me?" Pop asked.

"Not won't. Can't. He's propelled by his own narrative. It's his engine."

"So what will 'e do next?" Ma asked.

"He'll kill Jimbo. Unless we stop him."

Chapter XXVI

'The emotions of hatred, envy, covetousness and lust for domination [are] life-conditioning emotions…which must fundamentally and essentially be present in the total economy of life.'
Nietzsche

"You find my son, Mister Rook, and stop him, or I'll stop you. The civilized stage of our relationship is over. Now it's down and dirty. You do what I say," said Pop.

"It's not customary to kill your employees," I said.

"Think you're funny, bloody Aristotle, with all this butchering going on?" Ma said.

Pop smiled. "He jokes 'cos he's scared. His insides are jellied eels. It's a front. You're as much a bleedin' actor as poor Georgie is."

He was right. Everything I did was some sort of act, and I was very frightened. It was like a free drug. Also, there was something else about Georgie's intentions, but I didn't think it timely to tell them just now. Things were complicated enough.

"He said Jimbo would probably be at Spider's gaff. It's where he bought his snow and crack. Certainly the last time I spoke to Jimbo he was rapidly…" I whirled the air with my hand.

Pop and Ma looked at each other.

"Spider Morrison. Dino'll know the gaff. Let's go," Pop said.

Ma looked incredulous. "You? You ain't been out since the funeral."

"It's a family affair. The family'll finish it. We take two cars. Me and Rook in one, you in another, Dino driving."

"You know Georgie will be armed," I said.

"Then you better think of some clever bastard thing to say so he don't shoot you this time. Dino will be loaded anyway."

*

Forty five minutes later Pop was sitting beside me in a brand new Audi, his wheelchair in the boot. Ma and Dino were following.

"Drives like an angel, don't she?" said Pop, suddenly relaxing. It was a new experience to be in a car that almost drove itself. I could see that for all the mayhem in his family, it was moments like this that justified it all. You're rich, you're in a car that is like a bed of feathers and you're still alive after breaking, bending and reshaping all the rules. Mohammed Ali once said that if he had to make a choice again between being a Parkinsons-addled ex-champ who had his brains knocked about for half a lifetime or stay being a sign painter in Dallas, there's no choice at all. Pop made his own luck, got tough and dirty when he had to, and made a pile. He'd either done deals with or seen off the Americans, the Russians, the Bulgarians, the Chinese, and now had a global empire. I'd rather have a drink with a foxy, dangerous player like him than with a respectable financial consultant or banker who has just legally stolen a family pension. The Steele family was like a history of empires writ small: all the violent creativity and ruthless building and vision goes into expansion and consolidation, then things reach a zenith and, slowly or spectacularly, the whole carapace implodes. I was having these thoughts to avoid imagining what might soon be a scene of carnage. I knew the Steeles well enough by now to anticipate carnage and surprise rather than tea and conciliation.

Spider lived in a first floor Peabody Estate flat in Farringdon Lane in the old city, a spit from the Barbican. It wasn't glamorous. There are different stratas of dealers, just as there are in the rest of society – a few live in Bel Air and have private jets and at the other end there are those who sleep in bus shelters and eat yesterday's burgers from litter bins. Spider was top end of the bottom rung because at least he had a roof over his head. I spoke into the security panel.

"Here to see Spider. I'd like to score. I'm a friend of Jimbo Steele."

Spider obviously smelled a rat and jumped from a back window, straight into the loving arms of Dino, who marched him to the front, with Ma trailing. Pop stayed in the car. A few kids in mixed football strips – Arsenal, West Ham, Millwall, stopped kicking a ball and watched goggle-eyed as Spider fumbled with a key.

"Is Jimbo here?" Ma asked.

"Nah. Honest. Ain't seen him for months," said Spider. His flat smelled like a whore's handbag – sweet, jasminey and the thick yellow smell of hash. Bob Marley on the wall, garage booms on the iPod, probably nothing much in the fridge, SKY news silently on the wall TV. A baby crawled across a snot green carpet, jam encrusted lips and a toilet roll in one hand. A woman of about thirty going on seventy in tight jeans and a cheesecloth shirt encasing breasts like wet pasta shells ambled in.

"Shut up, sit down. Keep the baby schtum," said Mum. The young woman sat ignoring the baby, who was now happily absorbed chewing on a Lou Reed CD. Spider was surprisingly chubby – no bone-thin tattooed addict here, but a lardy lad with no chin, just a face that disappeared into folds of neck, and a New York Dodgers baseball cap over thin blond hair. He had too many teeth – all jockeying for position, and the eyes of a stricken fish. Ma looked at the woman.

"When was Jimbo here?" she asked.

"Yest'day. Went last night," she said before Spider could stop her.

Ma nodded at Dino and he took out his gun and hit Spider across the bridge of his nose. We all heard it crack and the blood started pumping immediately over the carpet. The baby looked at it amazed and started to clap. The woman paled and cringed on the sofa. Spider dropped to his knees and just let the blood pour.

"Did he say where he was going?"

"Look, I have an idea where…" I started but Ma slapped me hard around the face.

"We'll save your ideas for afters," she said, and looked back at Spider.

"I got no idea where…" Dino cracked him around the head, splitting an ear.

"Please. Honest. I dunno where…" and Dino cracked him in the jaw. Bits of teeth cascaded over the carpet. The baby's eyes sparkled and he or she gave a jammy grin from ear to ear.

"I think he's kosher," said Dino.

"Yeh," agreed Ma. "But give 'im a shock anyway."

Dino smashed open an electrical plug casing just above the floor until the wires were exposed, then he put on thin rubber gloves which he took from his pocket and grabbed Spider's left leg. He pulled off the trainer and a filthy yellowish sock. Spider's eyes locked in terror as he realised what was going to happen.

"No, no. Why? I ain't done nothing…" he spluttered through blood, snot and cracked teeth.

"This is for giving my boy the hard stuff," she said.

Dino jammed a toe in the open socket and Spider screamed. His whole fat body jerked and blubbered and his hands clawed at the carpet. The iPod fused and the TV spluttered and died. I could hear something electrical protest and squawk from a kitchen area. The old young woman curled up on the sofa, gnawing one set of knuckles in white fear. The baby was slowly, dimly beginning to realise that all was not rosy and started to whimper, then bawl. After what seemed like a holy age Spider stopped convulsing. I guess his heart had given out. Ma was looking at me, gauging my reaction. It was brutal, inhuman, unforgiving. Would she have done the same if I'd not been there? Probably.

As we left, Ma stooped and chucked the snivelling baby under the chin. "Nice kid," then at the mother, "should be ashamed, letting it get all this crap round its mouth. Manners starts early, girl. Oh, and don't forget, we were never here. Look after that baby. And keep it off the chips, then it won't end up a tub of lard like its old man."

Then we were gone.

Chapter XXVII

'Now is the dramatic moment of fate, Watson, when you hear a step upon the stair which is walking into your life, and you know not whether for good or ill.'

Arthur Conan Doyle

We sat in Farringdon Lane, Pop and I in the front, Ma and Dino in the back. It was a chilly, mackerel-sky, drizzly London day. Pop knew by my ashen face that something had happened.

"If Spider is no longer with us, due to some unforeseen and highly regrettable domestic tragedy, I trust there will be no loose ends," he said, sarcasm barely blanketing his anger.

"It's done. It's good to get out there and mix it a bit. Show people we're still mustard. But Socrates 'ere has another idea about Georgie. If it's as good as the last one we're in for a long bloody night."

Pop turned to me. "Now you've seen my wife in action you know it was her ladylike manner and Swiss finishing school decorum that first attracted me. Now talk."

"I think Jimbo may have gone to the factory. Georgie mentioned Spider's first as a likely place, but then he said something about going somewhere familiar and now Tony's gone…," I said.

"That's it?" said Ma. "That's your bleedin' brilliant idea?"

Pop turned his crocodile eyes on her. "And you've got a better one? Now you've topped someone your blood's up. Like a bleedin' harpy. The sheer bloody stupidity of taking out some crummy street arab when we're shitting money legally all over the world. I know you. God, I know you, woman…Now get in the other car!"

Ma and Dino got out and followed us. Pop was now in a thoroughly bad mood after a messy and unnecessary death and was presumably experiencing shipping forecast cold turkey. We all have our addictions.

At the factory we punched in the codes and drove in, parked, and then walked into the building, Dino first with his gun ready, Ma behind and Pop cruising in his wheelchair, like an ancient warlord in an electric chariot. I walked beside him. We stopped and faced the numerous aisles of goods collecting dust: tins of paints; Christmas decoration trash; cheap kitchen goods; a few dusty children's toys littered the aisles, including a clown with a leg and arm missing.

"Georgie! Georgie boy! It's Pop. Son, whatever's been done – let's talk. Georgie!"

Nothing. I looked at the toys on the shelves, like miniature dusty wax works. One looked cleaner. Noddy, but he was gaffer taped to a toy chair and his mouth was gagged. This was a message. Georgie certainly didn't lack gallows humour. I indicated the bizarre little figure to Pop, then pointed to the small offices where I'd found the girl. Our odd looking little band approached. One of the offices had dusty glass panels and inside Jimbo, eyes like red gobstoppers, was gaffer taped to a chair, his mouth taped too. Ma reached forward to open the door but I stopped her. The glass panelled door was filthy except for one spot near the top. I stood on tiptoe. A red wire was visible. Jimbo's eyes told me that he could see something from his side, an explosive device presumably. Georgie's strange odyssey had begun with a bomb planted by one of the family and he had decided he would end it the same way. I indicated this to Dino and he took over. Subtlety wasn't his strong point. He elbowed a pane of glass and it shattered satisfyingly. I ducked, thinking it might set off the explosive device, but nothing happened. Dino pushed the remaining glass out and climbed inside, then unwired the device and opened the door.

Jimbo was in a bad way: dehydrated, soaked in sweat, and presumably coming down from whatever he'd been taking since he left home. I took off the gaffer tape from his mouth and he gasped. Dino undid the rest and Ma started to massage some circulation back into his arms and legs. It was the first really maternal spontaneous thing I'd seen her do, and since less than two hours ago she'd viciously tortured and murdered a young man, making his wife a widow and leaving his baby fatherless, it didn't really go far in balancing the moral compass.

"I come down here just to get a bit of peace. I must have conked out and when I woke up I was trussed up and could see the explosive on the door. I didn't even see no one. I got no idea who done it," he said.

Ma looked at Pop. The time for cover ups was over.

"Your brother did it, son," said Pop.

Jimbo looked baffled. His brothers were all dead, as far as he knew.

"Georgie's alive. It's him who...did this," Pop said, waving his hand as if painting in the air vivid images of all recent carnage.

Jimbo looked at Ma, then at me. "Is this true?"

I nodded. "I've seen him, talked to him. Ma too. It's a long story."

"We've 'ad enough for one day. Let's get home," said Ma.

Jimbo struggled to his feet with some difficulty. He took my arm and we started to walk down one of the aisles. For one of the richest crime families in the world, we looked a depleted band of ragamuffins in search of a bed. Jimbo was trying to reassemble what was left of his brain and puzzle things out.

"So it was Georgie who…? Christ. What the hell happens now?"

Even before I looked up I knew he was there.

"What happens now, little bro', is me. You need more than guts to be a good gangster, you need ideas."

Another Cagney line. Georgie stood at the far end of the aisle. Dino still had his gun but was unsure what to do. He looked at Pop, who raised a hand to suggest we take this calmly.

"It's good to see you, son," said Pop.

Georgie looked uneasy. My contact with him had told me that he didn't like expressions of feeling head on, but preferred to talk obliquely, through imaginary scenes and films, unless it was on his terms and of his choosing.

"Bada bing, Popsicle. Long time no see," he said.

"You could've come to me, Georgie," said Pop.

"Natural law. Sons are put on this earth to trouble their fathers," said Georgie. Pop didn't realise it was a line Paul Newman has in *Road to Perdition*.

"Georgie. Why'd you do it? And why me? I never hurt you. We got along, didn't we?" asked Jimbo. This was the wrong way to go about defusing Georgie. He started to look increasingly ruffled. His hand tightened on the gun. He was liable to start shooting.

"I don't mind if you don't like my manners, I don't like them myself. They are pretty bad. I grieve over them on long winter evenings," he said.

"Bogart," I said. "I stick my neck out for nobody,"

"Whenever you try to do the right thing, you always get kicked in the face," said Georgie, quoting Cagney and happier now we were trading quotations.

"Both born in 1899," I said.

"Manhattan, but different sides of the street," said Georgie.

"Tough, feisty, aggressive Cagney. His father was a bartender; his mother was the daughter of a barge captain."

"Bogie's father was a surgeon, his mother a successful commercial artist. Chalk and cheese."

"Yet they ended up in the same place."

"But different. Cagney – proactive, comes out fighting, chip on his shoulder."

"Bogie – cool, laconic, a slow burner."

Georgie visibly relaxed. Pop looked at me with a respectful smile. Almost. It was then that it all went wrong. It was the smile that did it.

Chapter XXVIII

'Choose something you love and then let it kill you.'

Charles Bukowski

Georgie tenses and wires up instantly. He stares at Pop who is still smiling, now at him, but less certain. Jimbo's hands shake and he needs a fix of something to calm him. Ma stares at Georgie. Pop doesn't know what he's done to antagonize his son.

"You think I'm funny?" asks Georgie.

"No Georgie, I don't think you're funny," says Pop.

"You're smiling. Hell, something's funny. Is it my face? These scars. The scars on your son's face? So you can share a joke with this dick who isn't even family? This Rooky. A joke about me?"

"No, Georgie, it was just the Bogart and Cagney stuff."

"You find them funny then. You find Jimmy Cagney's cocky, whaddaya-hear-whaddaya-say in your face strut amusing? One of the great cinema icons of the twentieth century. He's just a joke to you? And Bogie's introverted, obsessing loner – that's a screamer too? Both outsiders. Rebels. You find them hilarious?"

"No, Georgie. I don't."

"So it's back to me, then. You mean, let me understand this cos', ya know maybe it's me, I'm a little fucked up maybe, but I'm funny how, I mean funny like I'm a clown, I amuse you? I make you laugh, I'm here to fuckin' amuse you? What do you mean funny, funny how? How am I funny?"

Georgie is in *Goodfellas* now. I try to placate him with the next line: "Just... you know, how you tell the story. What?" But Georgie isn't having it. He stabs the gun towards Pop as he speaks, saliva dripping down his chin. His bad eye is almost closed in rage.

"No, no Rooky. Let him speak."

"You know I love you, son," says Pop.

"No, no, I don't know. How do I know? You said I'm funny. How the fuck am I funny, what the fuck is so funny about me? Tell me, tell me what's funny!"

Perhaps in his hyperventilating rage, and because of his impaired vision, he doesn't see properly, and thinks Dino is going for his gun, when all he is doing is running his hand through his hair, wondering what to do, but Georgie shoots him three times in quick succession. The third shot must have hit a bone and flips Dino off his feet. He hits the ground and his left leg twitches involuntarily, his jeans dampening where he wet himself. Being shot is not a slomo aesthetic experience. It is horribly visceral and the spouting blood quickly pollutes your nostrils and you want to be sick.

"Shouldn't have reached for it," says Georgie.

"He wasn't!" says Jimbo.

"Shut it, bro!" and Georgie shoots Jimbo in the shoulder. He falls across Pop's lap, blood pumping over the pair of them. For a moment Georgie wavers, but then the doors open in his head and all hell breaks loose. Full carnage in his eyes. He's gone.

"What the hell, I might as well do you all."

He aims at Ma but before he can squeeze the trigger he looks startled and reels into a pile of boxed Barbie dolls, which come crashing down on him. At the far end of the aisle is Philly with the gun Ma placed in her room. She looks at it, amazed at what she has just done, and drops the gun. I run down the aisle to where Georgie fell. There are bleeding Barbie dolls everywhere, like being in some weird boutique abortion clinic, tiny bodies and broken boxes, but no Georgie. I follow the blood trail through kitchen towels and office supplies and find him sprawled in garden ornaments among dozens of smiling gnomes. The bullet caught him just right of the spine above the stomach. It has probably shattered his liver and he has minutes rather than hours. I kneel beside him.

"You want me to get a doctor?"

He smiles. "I don't need no doctor. I need a director. Tell me what's happening."

"OK. It's a shootout. Final scene."

"Who's there?"

"You. Central role. All your buddies taken out by the cops and the dirty rat who double crossed you."

"What's his name?"

"Jimmy the Mole, on account of he's a snitch, but he's also got a mole the size of a plum on his cheek."

"That's good," Georgie says, half smiling. "How many cops?"

"A dozen. Jimmy set you up here, but you winged the rat and now you're hunting him through this place while the cops hunt you. You've taken three of them out but dirty yellow rat Jimmy got you from behind. It's bad. You stagger down one aisle, then another. A cop appears. You take a pop and wing him, then crash through the boxes to another aisle. You see a tailcoat vanish around the corner. You crash through another aisle and there he is. Jimmy the Mole facing you. He squeezes the trigger but you're quicker and he gets it smack between the eyes."

"Smack between the eyes. Good. But the cops?"

"Swarming like ants. There are more now. Twenty cops, and they close in. You get one, then two…but the odds are stacked and you take another hit in the leg, the arm, your gun spins away and you turn to face them, fire still in your eye and you say…"

"Made it, Ma! Top of the world!"

"And then there's a storm of lead…"

His good eye looks at something behind me, then glitters for a moment before smoking over and it is done. I turn around and Ma is standing there.

*

I didn't tell the Steeles that this had to happen, that we were in a classical drama where inevitability has to unfold events to a tragic end. Georgie couldn't walk from a classic gangster movie where he'd been living for five years into a family soap opera – he'd typecast himself. We took Jimbo to the private clinic the family used. Being shot might be the best thing to happen to him if he cleans up too, but I doubt he'll do that. The family has the black spot on it. I went back to the house and Pop and I shared a morose scotch. He paid me, with a bonus, which seemed ironic. Philly retreated to a fug of smoke, bad music and broken dreams. Presumably someone took away Dino's body to be ignominiously dumped. Ma seemed to have shrunk before my eyes. When I left she was furiously nibbling a garibaldi and staring at a blank wall. As I left Pop's room he suddenly abandoned his own thoughts and entered mine.

"You've seen my family turn into piranhas. You've never said nothing about your parents. They gone?"

"My mother's gone. Though technically she is still alive. My father – I don't know. He wasn't averse to bending the law himself. One day I'll find the bastard."

"Maybe he'll find you," said Pop.

It was a thought. I was left to return to the confused wheels of my other life. And the bright spot that was Cass. And a little unfinished business to attend to.

Chapter XXIX

'I gladly come back to the theme of the absurdity of our education.'

Montaigne

He should have known better. Jeremy couldn't resist. He had to come in and see what would happen. I think the Prozac he was now on had given him a little sang froid, a bit of nerve. I'd accessed the most recent counselling file on him, which said: "The medication is helping Jeremy Tregown to function on a practical level, and Dr. Rook's absences from the university have perhaps given him a respite by removing the constant source of imaginary irritation. However, I believe he is still deeply troubled and liable to psychotic behaviour. I suggest his duties be reduced to purely administrative ones for the time being. Prolonged contact with others is not advisable, and students must be protected." It was time to give those psychotic behaviours a little prod.

It was my first lecture on the Philosophy and Religion module that Jeremy foolishly imagined would be a torment to me. A moment's serious reflection would have alerted him to potential dangers. I considered that whatever happened, he deserved it. I was almost curious as to what would happen myself. He sat at the back. I counted sixty one students seated attentively, including the beloved Cass. I'd had two glasses of Rioja and a small Famous Grouse. I was, for the first time in years, actually looking forward to performing this nonsense.

I looked at the massed faces and furrowed my brow to create the illusion of thought and seriousness.

"Philosophy and Religion. As some of you know I have a firm belief in the practical application of ideas. So, for the duration of this course I thought the best way to examine how religious belief systems operate would be to actually create and practice a religion. A new one. Then, at the end of the course, we'll scrutinise the whole project and everyone's essay can be based on the experience.

"Many faith systems are based on the deifying of a personality – Jesus, Mohammed – so in effect they constitute a personality cult. Even good old Satan has his own religious following, and let's admit it: Satan has really kept Christianity in business long past its sell by date. He's vital, energetic, charismatic, and refuses to play by the rules. Hell, I'd go for a drink with him over Saint Paul any day."

A few smiles. At least I had their attention. Jeremy was still smiling in his Prozac induced little Narnia at the back. I had my PowerPoint slides all primed.

"If you recall, the Imperial cult of the Roman Caesars defined them as gods; kings and queens even today are idealized, made heroic, and, at times given a god-like public image, often through unquestioning flattery and praise. Marx first coined the term 'personality cult' in 1877, but it's been around for thousands of years. If we look at how these cults operate we may discover a great deal about how religions function. Many political movements are quasi-religious in that there is an active invention on the part of the leaders themselves to create a smoke and mirrors halo of divinity, self-glorification, and holy purpose. These things are, of course, a mask for narcissistic and monstrous egotism, vanity, pride, and selfishness. People who have lost touch, or been allowed to lose touch, with their mutable and flawed humanity. They are monsters."

Here I showed slides of Hitler, Nicolae Ceausescu, Caligula, Ayatollah Khomeini, Stalin, and finally Jeremy. There was a collective gasp and a few titters. Jeremy's smile froze into a glacial mask.

"These individuals usually exhibit inflated self-importance, tireless self-promotion, bragging, intense vanity, recklessness and probably have some form of sexual problem – inadequacy, impotence, a confusion of the penis with the whole body in some cases. These are the runts of humanity elevated beyond their intelligence and ability. They cannot cope with failure and try to destroy anyone or thing that they, in their delusional fantasies, believe is an enemy. Now you're probably wondering why, in this little gallery of trolls, I have included Jeremy Tregown, our illustrious Head of Department. As the Head, it seemed appropriate that we should designate him as our Godhead for this little social and philosophical experiment. Obviously not for a moment am I suggesting that Jeremy really exhibits any of the characteristics I have outlined. Is he vain, calculating, in a permanent rage against the world, inadequate, pompous, bitter hearted and spiritually vacuous? Of course not, you all cry. His cheerful bonhomie, generosity of spirit and legendary sense of humour are the very qualities that will allow him to be our mock deity for the next ten weeks. I am sure he will embrace what is merely a role with an educational purpose, with his usual gusto and even handedness."

All eyes were on Jeremy. He wanted to kill me so desperately you could smell it: bad onions and clogged drains. His nostrils dilated, his lips white slipping into blue. I hadn't finished yet. Not by a long chalk. I was just getting warmed up.

"So, how do we go about creating our Jeremy faith? First, we need to endow our icon with supernatural powers and a few miracles. Like so…" I brought up a slide, created with the help of Photoshop, of Jeremy in a long flowing white robe, a long white beard and rock star long hair, looking like Billy Connolly on amphetamines and snake juice, holding up a mighty staff which appeared to have stopped a tsunami in its tracks; another slide which showed Jeremy seated like Charlton Heston as Moses on a rock in a wilderness apparently conversing with aliens, who all looked like an ET nursery class; another of a sick woman hurling away her crutches as she skips towards her healing Messiah Jeremy who holds out his arms to her.

"We have already started a mythology. As believers we accept the veracity of these pictures as representations of the truth. Now we need some simple gestures which acknowledge Jeremy as a super being. Perhaps every time you see him, in the car park or the corridor, get on one knee and bow your head and mutter 'For I am blessed to see Jeremy.'"

Jeremy managed to rise from his seat and walk stiff legged from the room.

"What else do we need?" I asked.

"Prayers," said a spotty lad with no chin.

"Good, you can organize a daily prayer meeting in worship of his Holiness, Jeremy. I need a few people with a poetic bent to write some prayers?"

A few hands went up.

"We need some hymns or songs," said a chubby girl with ringlets. I made her chief hymn composer. Others were chosen to create icons, others still to invent prophecies that the mighty Jeremy had made.

"Shouldn't we crucify him? You know, like make him a martyr?"

"Martyrdom is excellent for promoting a myth, but crucifixion is against the Law. What you could do is make an effigy of Jeremy which you crucify, and then when he comes to work the next day you can organize a mass meeting in the car park to celebrate the fact that He is Risen from the dead," I said, getting a little carried away.

This was cooking nicely, when suddenly the doors swung open and things happened very quickly. Jeremy came in brandishing a cricket bat. He was still smiling, but his eyes looked strange, as if he wasn't really seeing anything in proper focus. He approached me at the lectern, raised the bat and took an almighty swing. I ducked in time and the bat smashed into the lectern. A girl screamed. A few students who had been smiling, thinking it a bizarre part of the lecture, suddenly stopped. Jeremy raised the bat again and swung wildly. I moved out of reach and he whirled round, lost his balance and fell over. In a sitting position he smashed the bat on the ground, where it broke and he sat looking dumbly at the rubber-bound handle. He seemed dazed and looked around, as if surprised to find himself there. Cass was now at my side.

"Dad – for God's sake get out before he does something else," she said.

I had a strong sense that we needed a grown up here, a responsible person to make decisions and create order. Then two men arrived, one I recognised as a beefy ex-rugby wing half who now taught something called *Project Reinvention Management*. He approached Jeremy quietly and said, "It's all right. We're here to help you," then pounced on Jeremy, got him in a powerful arm lock, tried to lift him and the two somehow fell over and rolled around the floor like two strange copulating creatures. My work was done here. All in all, a successful lecture.

*

I took Cass to dinner. We laughed a lot, then she went on to see an old school friend. I went to Anna's and we had sweet sex on her couch. Jimbo called me to say Pop had had another heart attack. I went home and opened a bottle of Famous Grouse. I had a phone message from the hospital asking when I would be visiting my mother. Three emails asking

Rook to call back about work – one was a drug dealer whose daughter had been raped and murdered by a rival, and the second a businessman whose partner had embezzled him, but he wanted him found and would then deal with him outside the Law. More and more people wanted to take things into their own hands and who can blame them? The third was a petty criminal who said he had proof the Royal Family was behind at least three murders – he wanted to go public but needed advice on the evidence he had amassed. I'd probably call the first back – no one should lose a daughter like that. Two hours later I telephoned Lizzie and left a message on her answerphone saying I loved her and wanted her back. It was an incredibly stupid thing to do which I would regret in the morning. First, I had the night to get through.

Printed in Great Britain
by Amazon